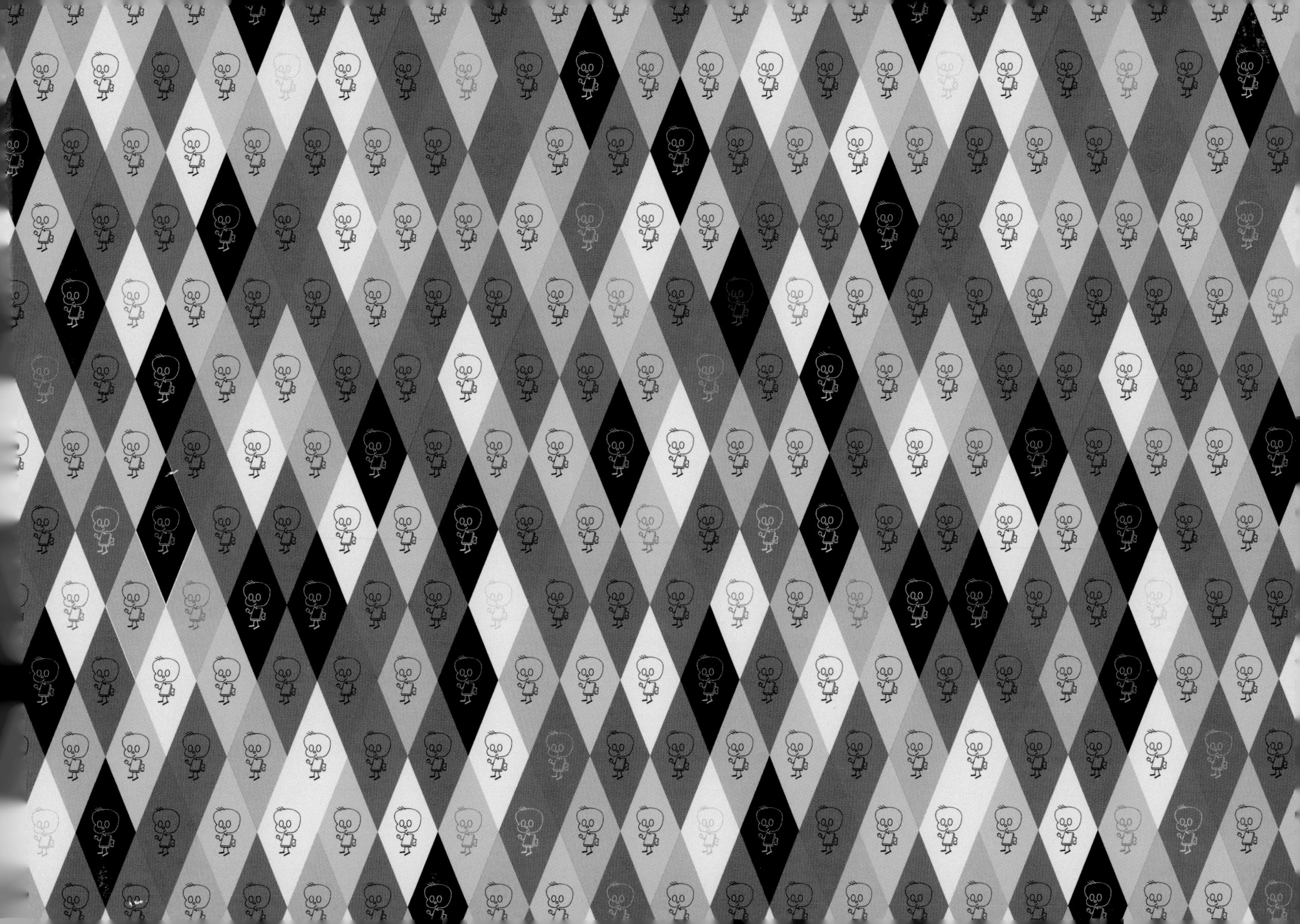

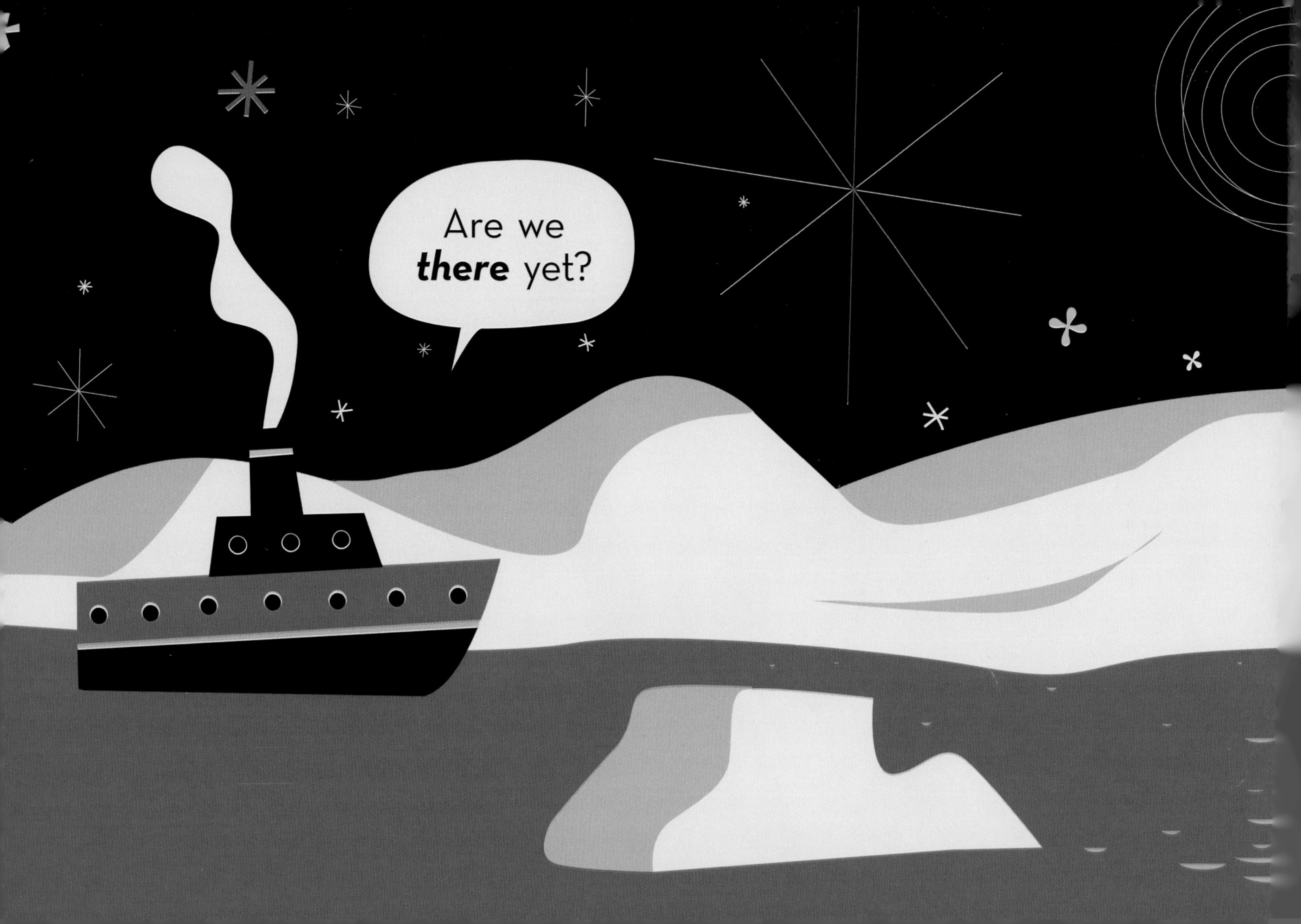
Are we **there** yet?

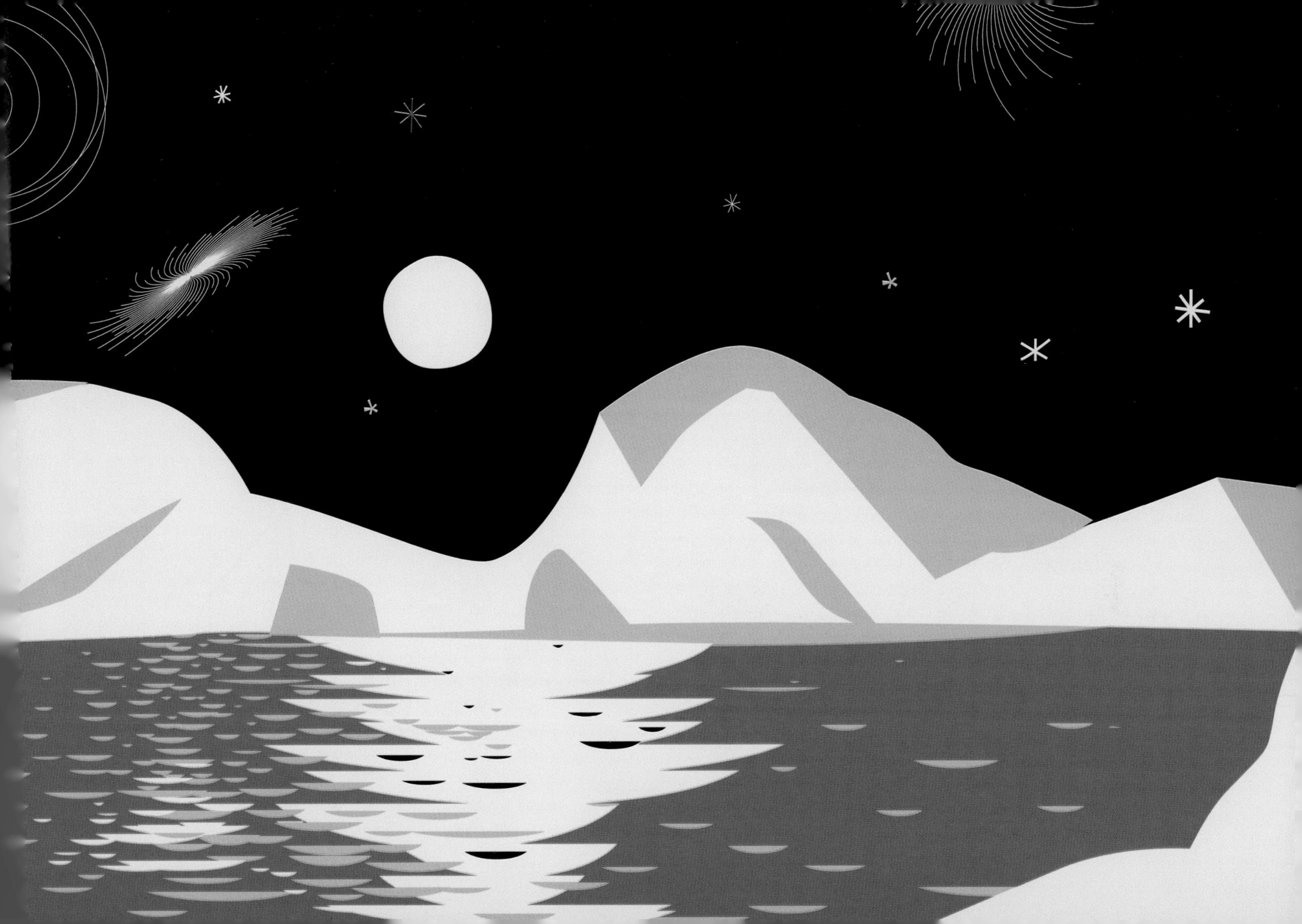

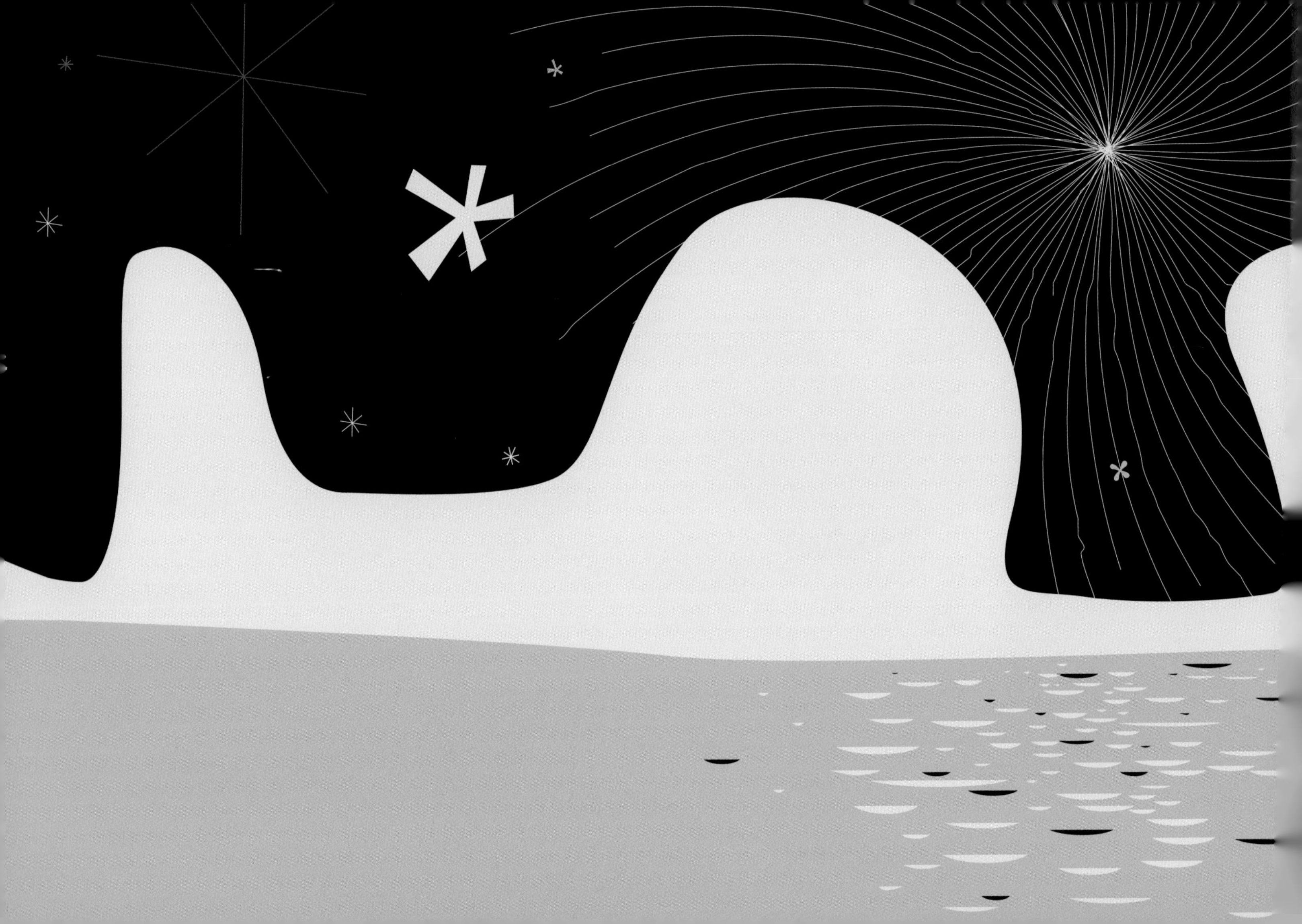

Soon, Mouse.

A TRIP TO THE BOTTOM OF THE WORLD

With Mouse

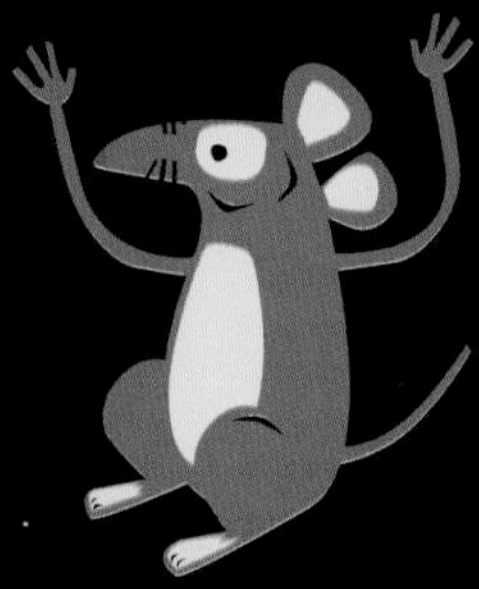

A TOON BOOK

By Frank Viva

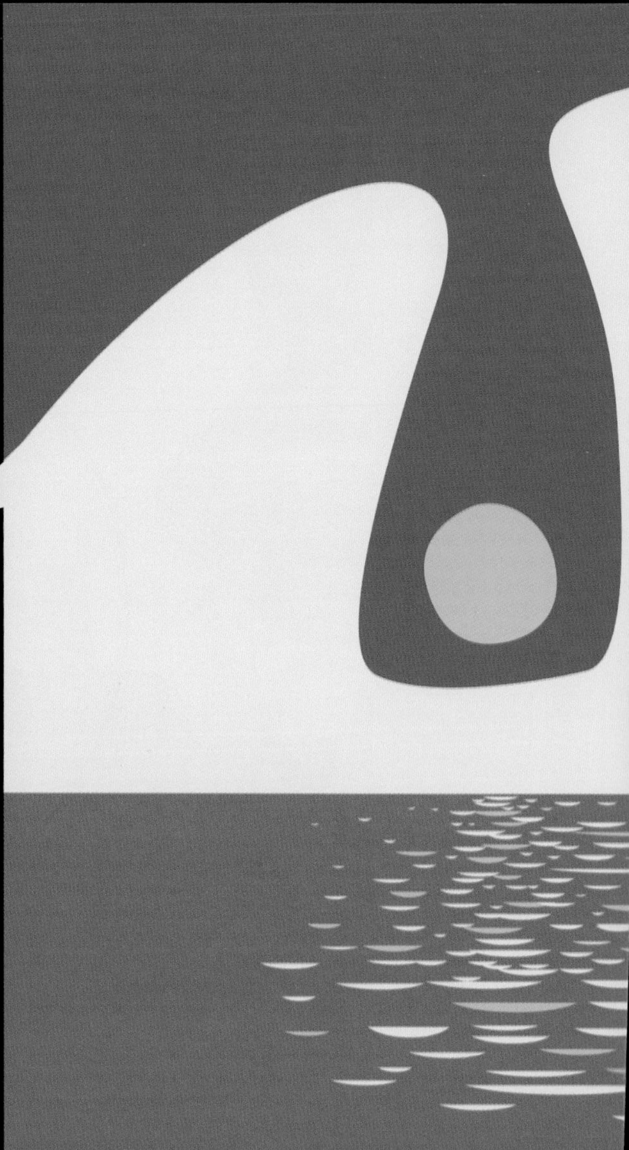

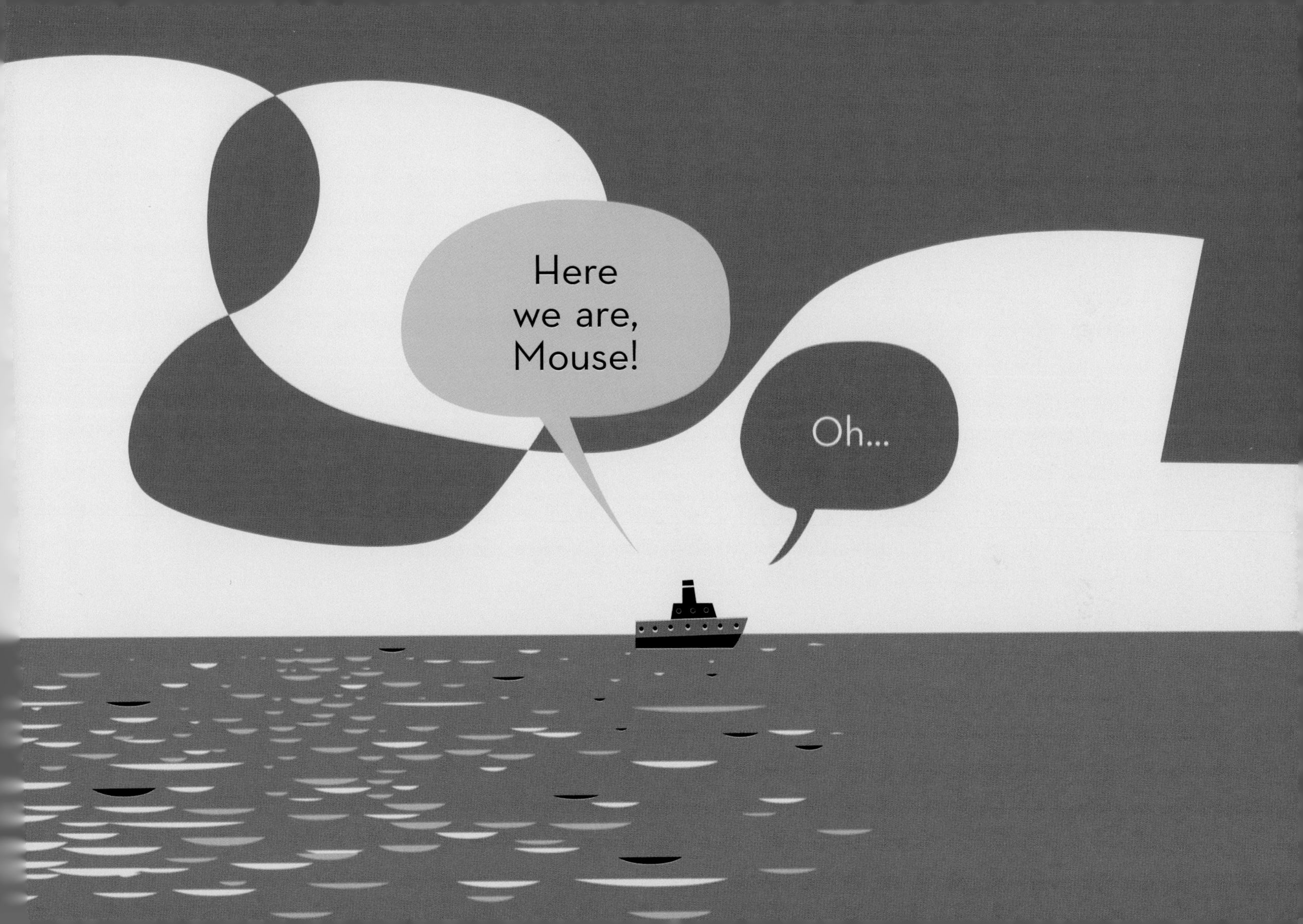
Here we are, Mouse!
Oh...

For Mouse and all the other pets I have had the pleasure to know.

Editorial Director: FRANÇOISE MOULY • Guest Editor: NADJA SPIEGELMAN • Book Design: FRANK VIVA and FRANÇOISE MOULY
FRANK VIVA's artwork was created using Adobe Illustrator. The words are set in Neutraface, and the display type is hand drawn by Frank Viva.

ABDOPUBLISHING.COM

Reinforced library bound edition published in 2016 by Spotlight, a division of ABDO, PO Box 398166, Minneapolis, Minnesota 55439.
Spotlight produces high-quality reinforced library bound editions for schools and libraries. Published by agreement with TOON Books.

Printed in the United States of America, North Mankato, Minnesota.
092015   012016

THIS BOOK CONTAINS
RECYCLED MATERIALS

WWW.TOON-BOOKS.COM

LIBRARY OF CONGRESS CATALOGING-IN-PUBLICATION DATA

This book was previously cataloged with the following information:

Viva, Frank.
 A trip to the bottom of the world with Mouse / Frank Viva.
  p. cm.
Summary: A boy and a mouse take a bumpy sea journey to the majestic expanses of the Antarctic, where they see the sights and meet new friends.
ISBN 978-1-935179-19-1
1. Graphic novels. [1. Graphic novels. 2. Antarctica--Fiction. 3. Animals--Antarctica--Fiction. 4. Mice--Fiction.]
I. Title.
PZ7.7.V59Tr 2012
741.5'973--dc23
                2011049499

ISBN 978-1-61479-428-8 (reinforced library bound edition)

Spotlight
A Division of ABDO
abdopublishing.com

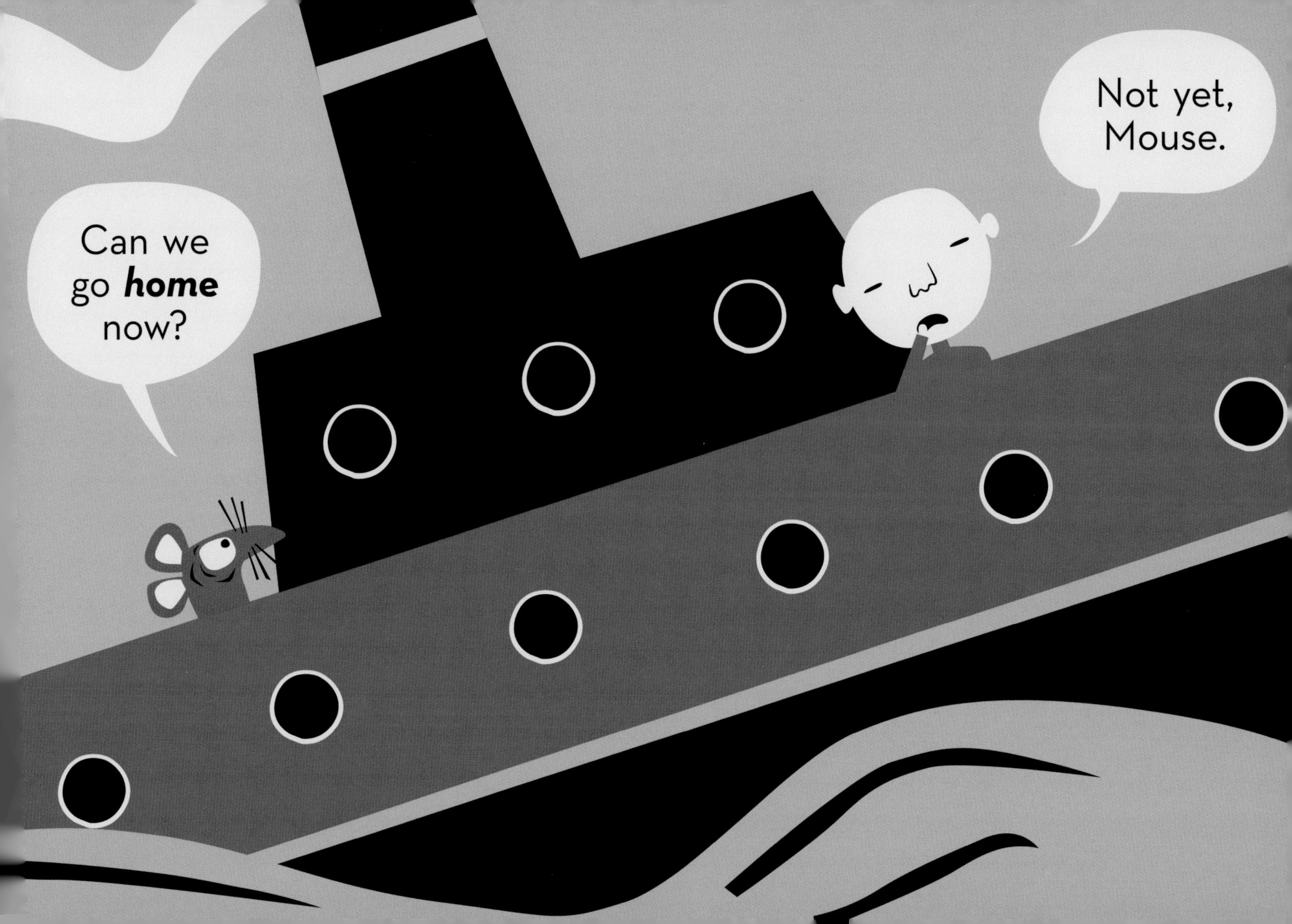

Can we go ***home*** now?
Not yet, Mouse.

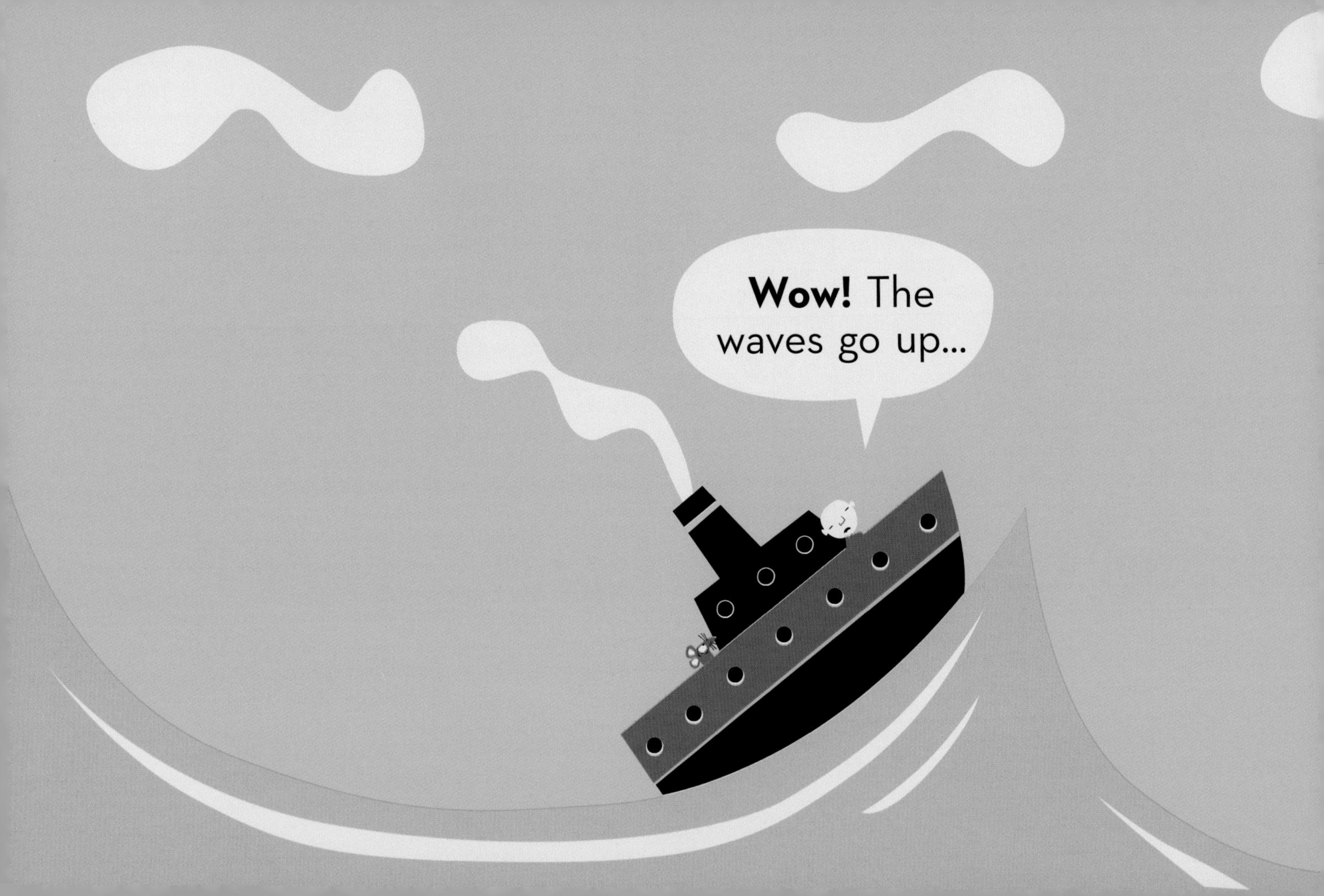
Wow! The waves go up...

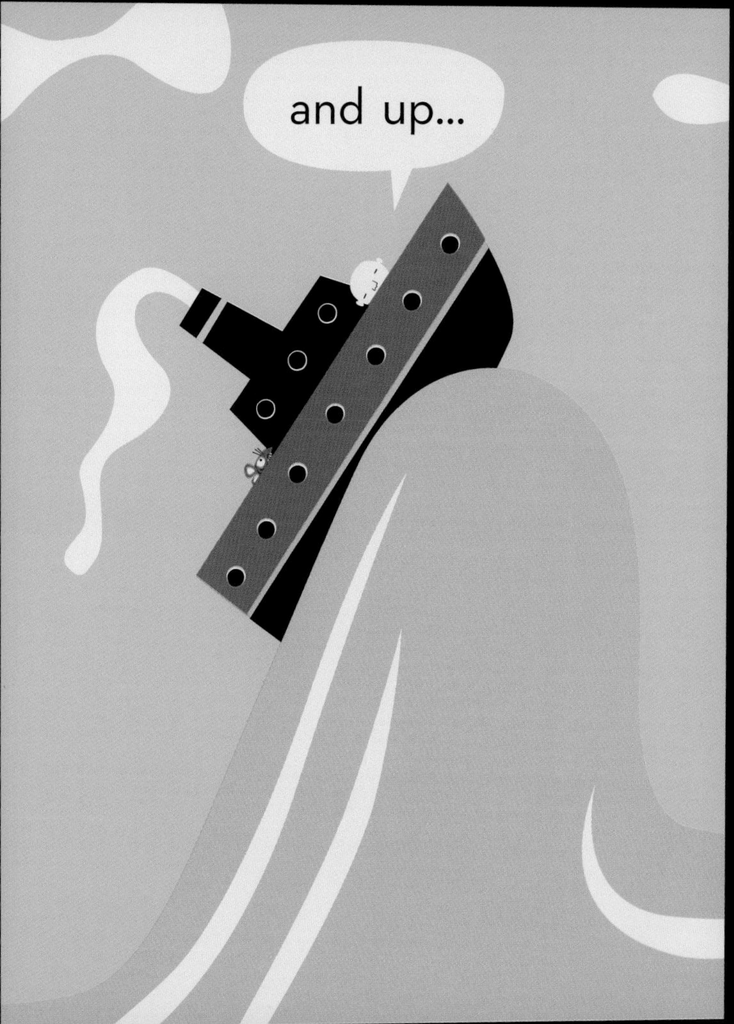
and up...

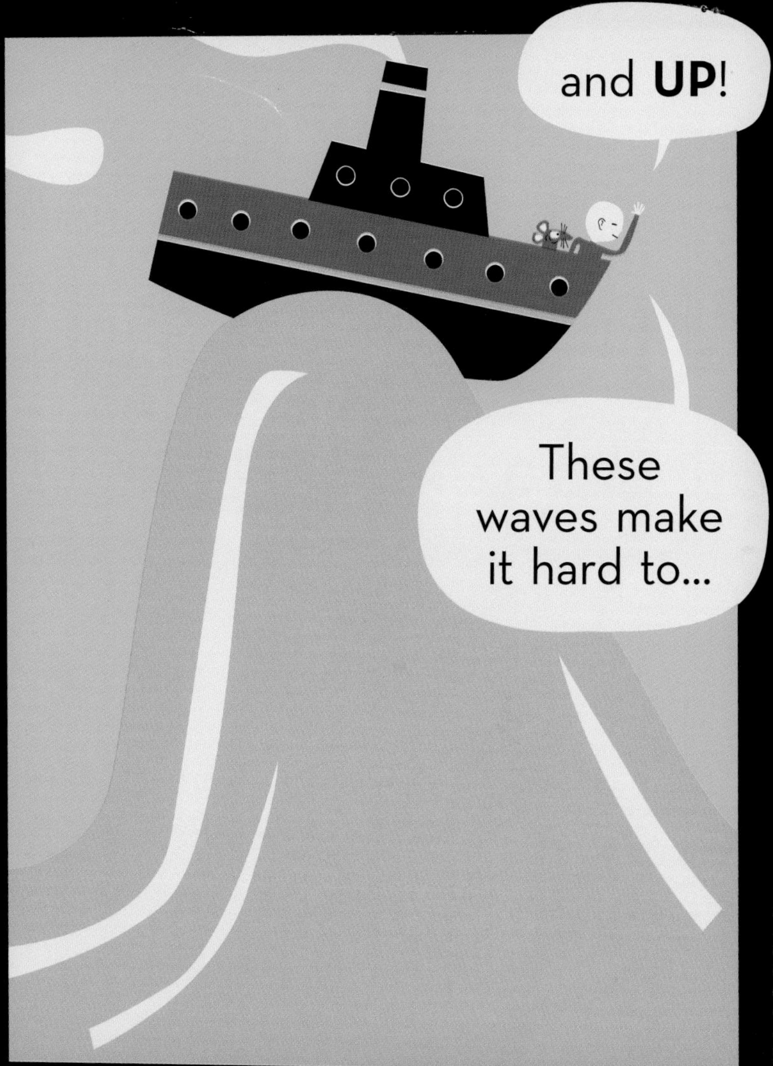
and **UP**!
These waves make it hard to...

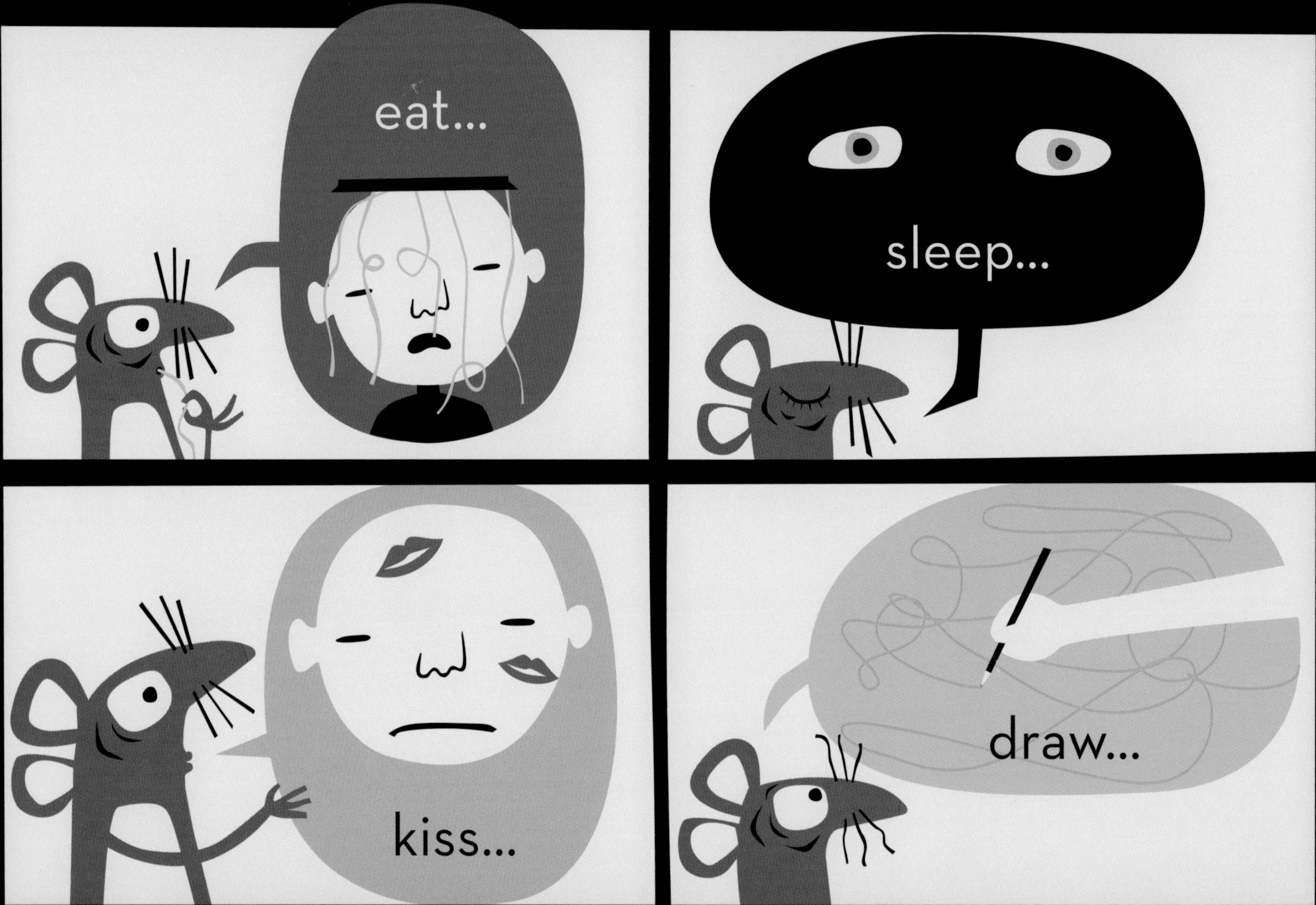
eat...
sleep...
kiss...
draw...

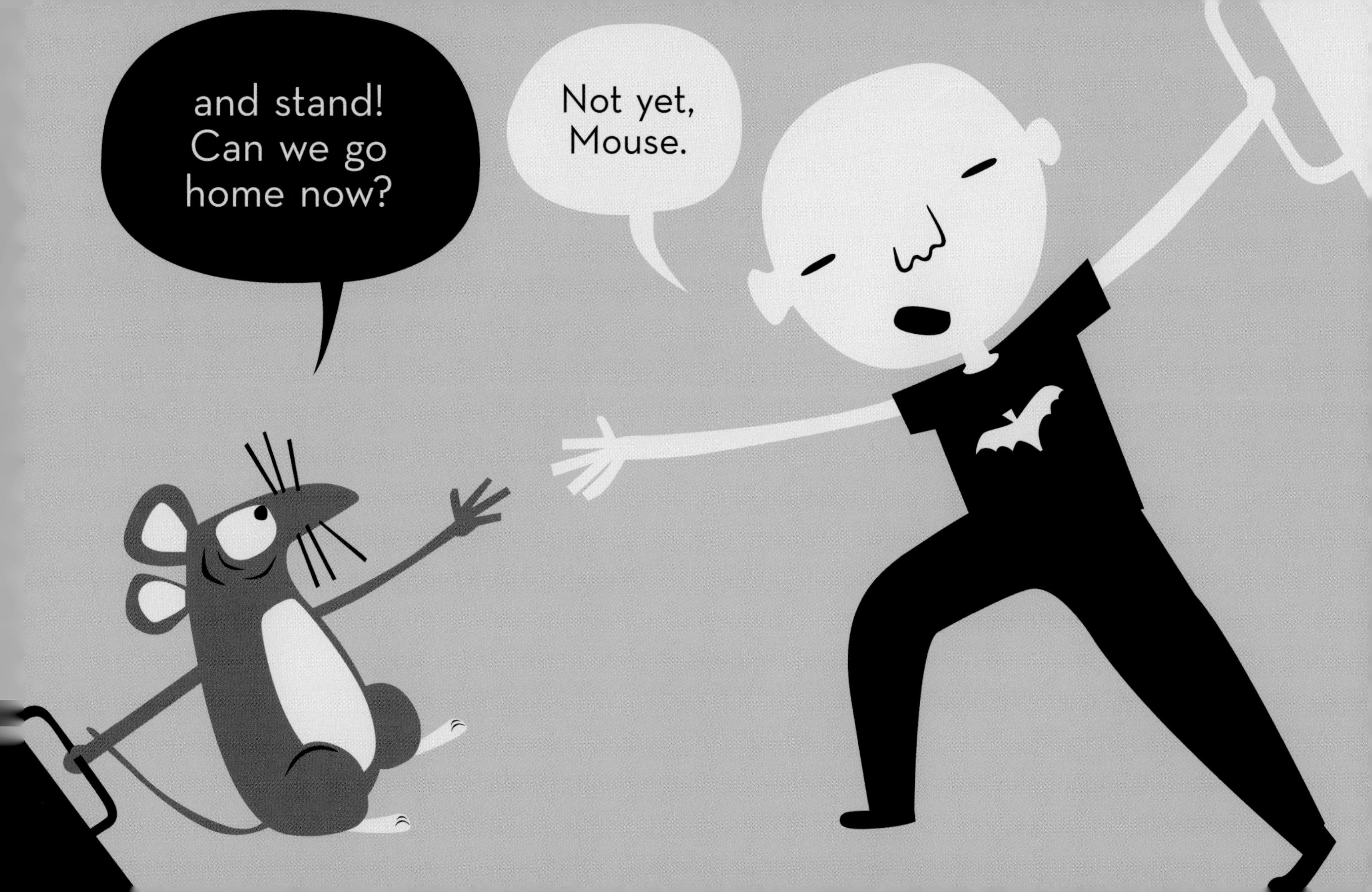
and stand! Can we go home now?
Not yet, Mouse.

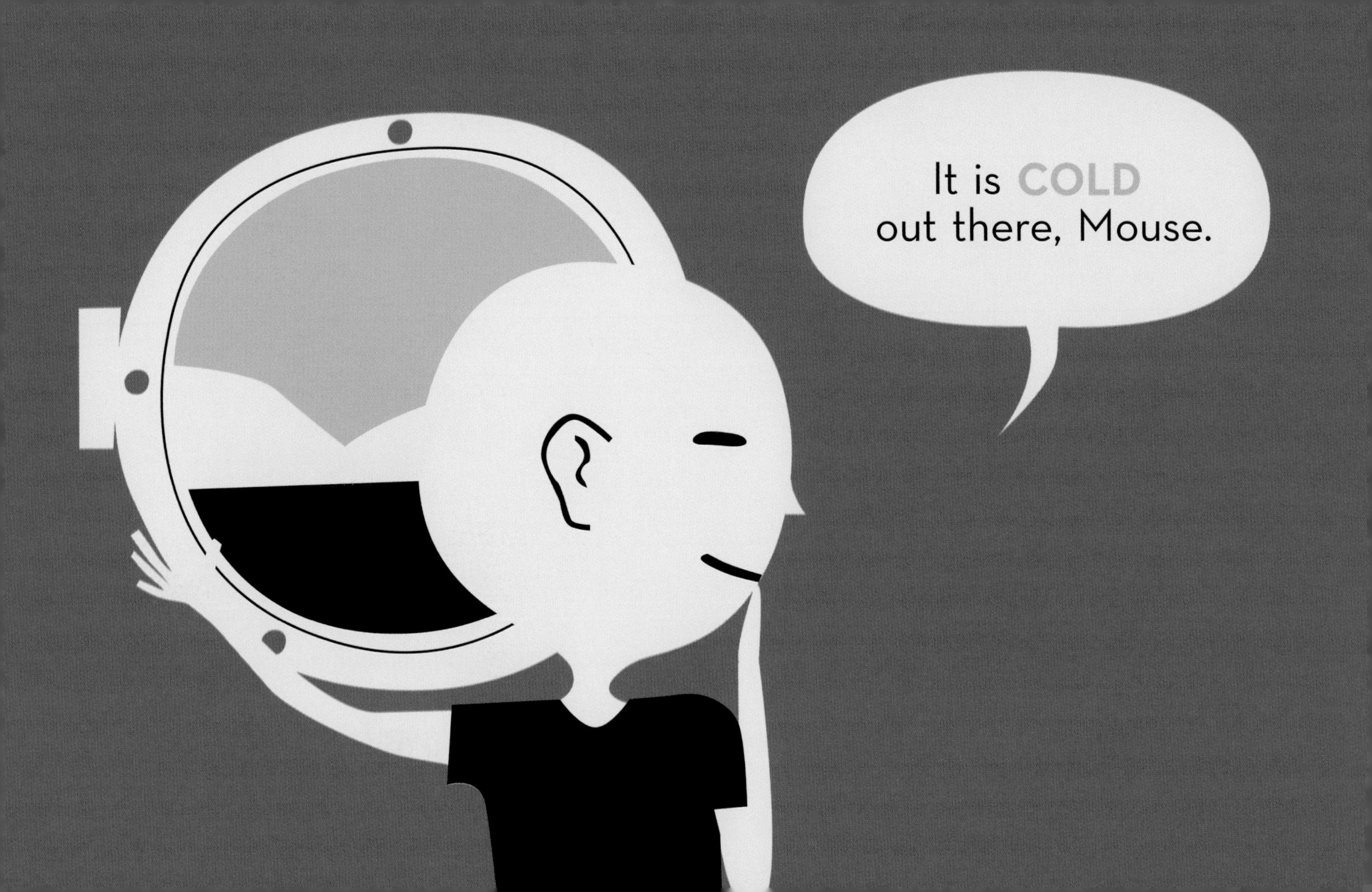
It is COLD out there, Mouse.

Then you
will need...

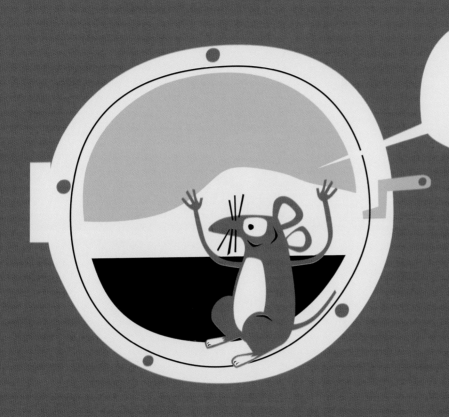

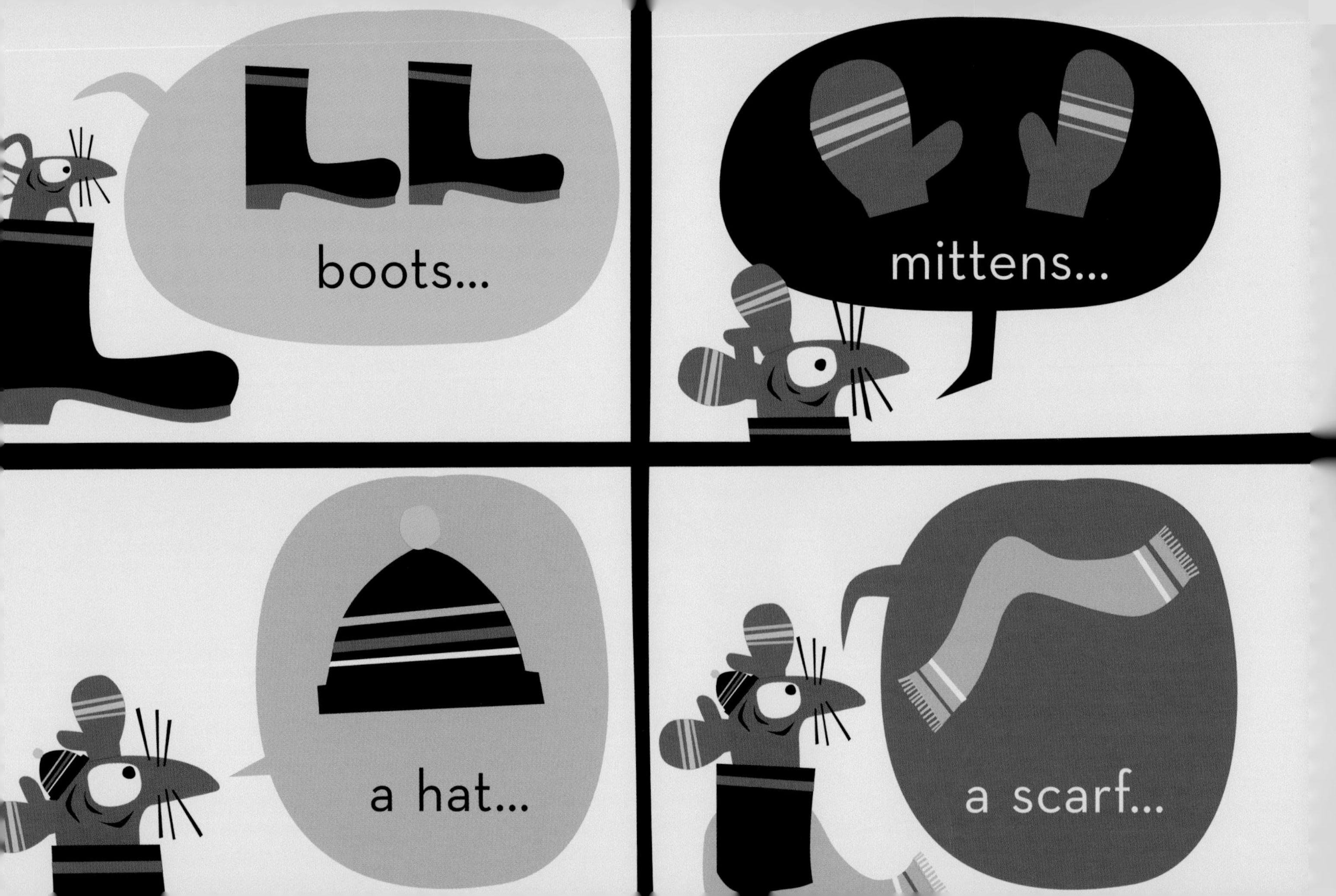
boots...
mittens...
a hat...
a scarf...

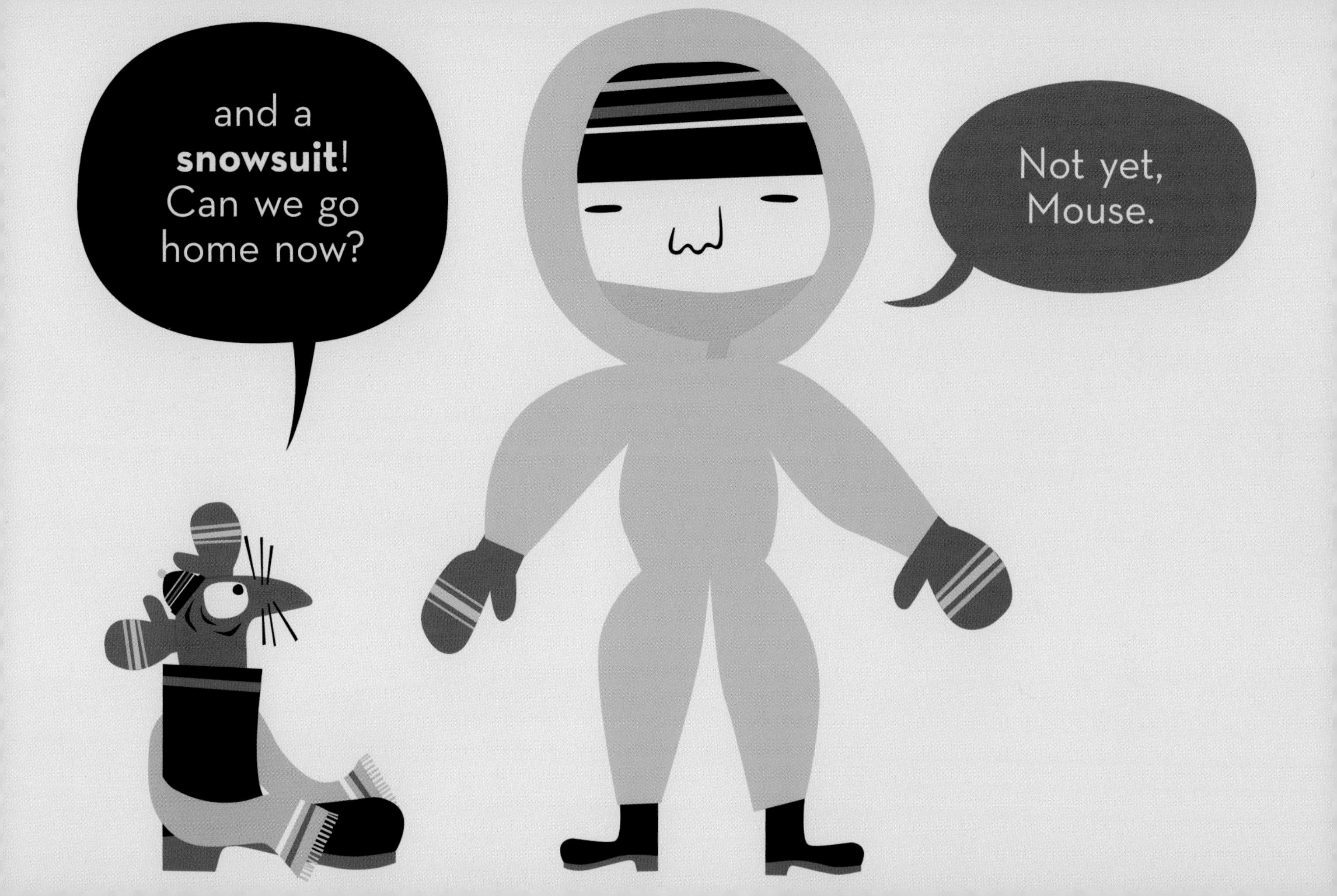
and a **snowsuit**! Can we go home now?
Not yet, Mouse.

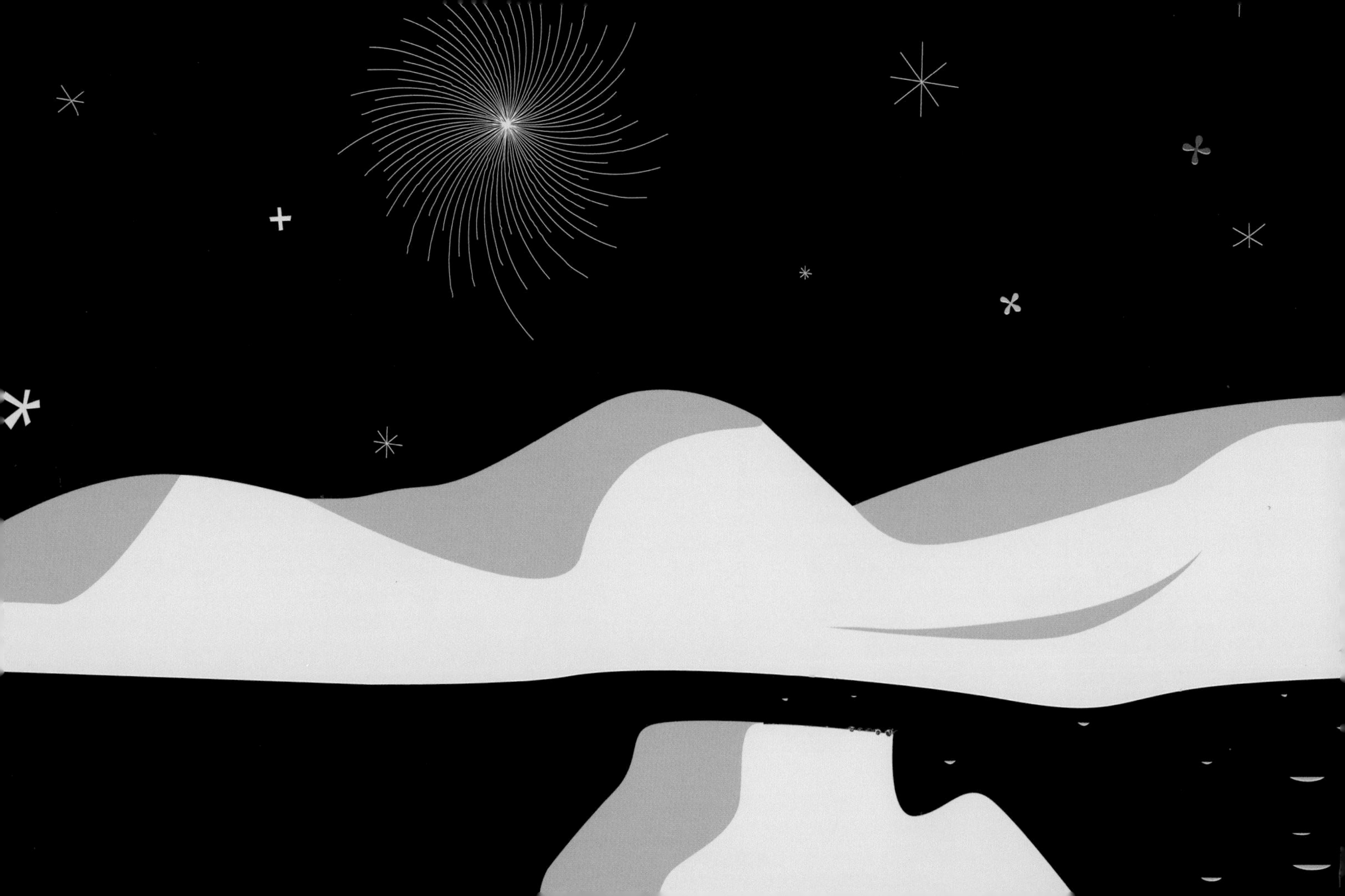

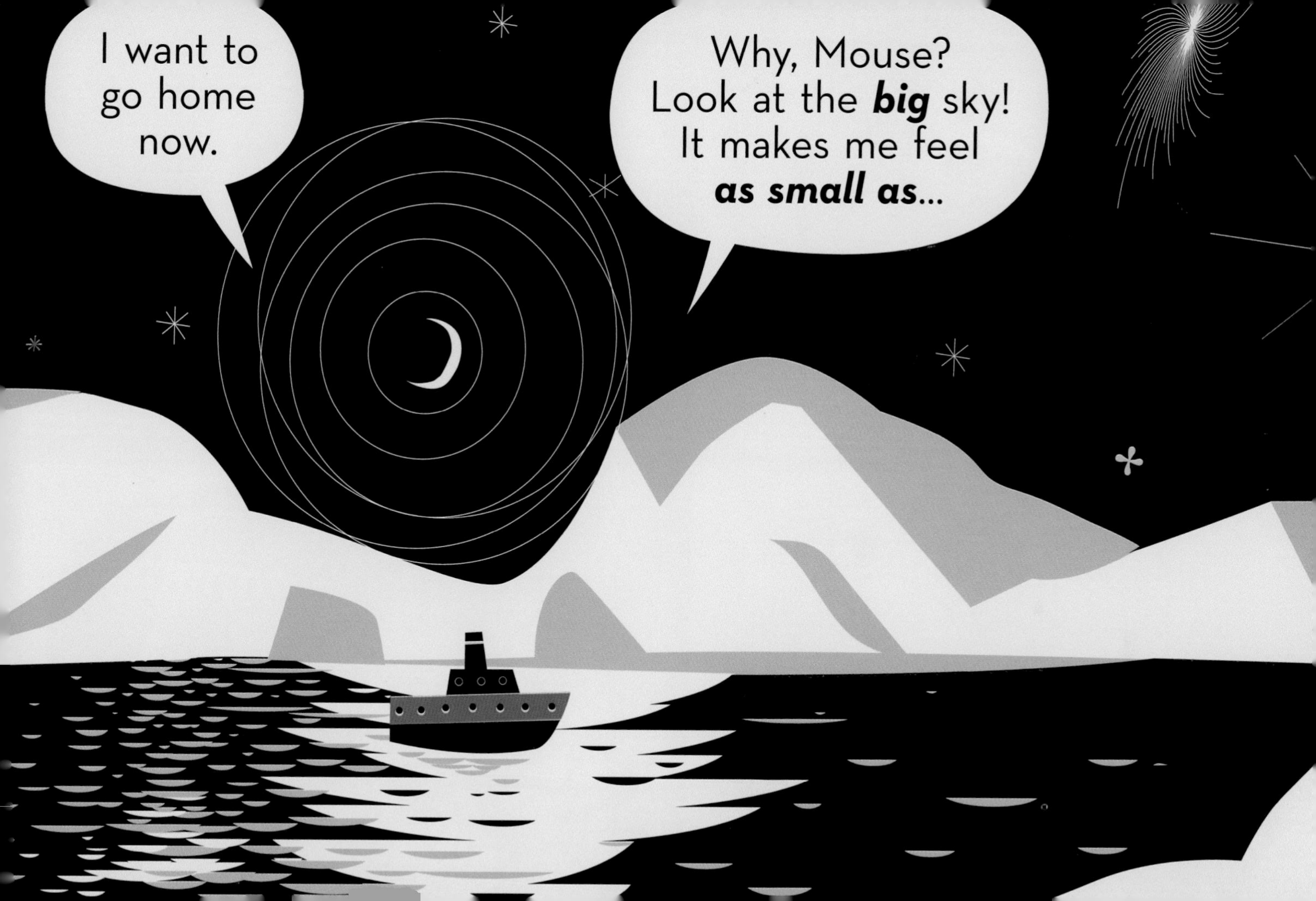
I want to go home now.
Why, Mouse? Look at the big sky! It makes me feel as small as...

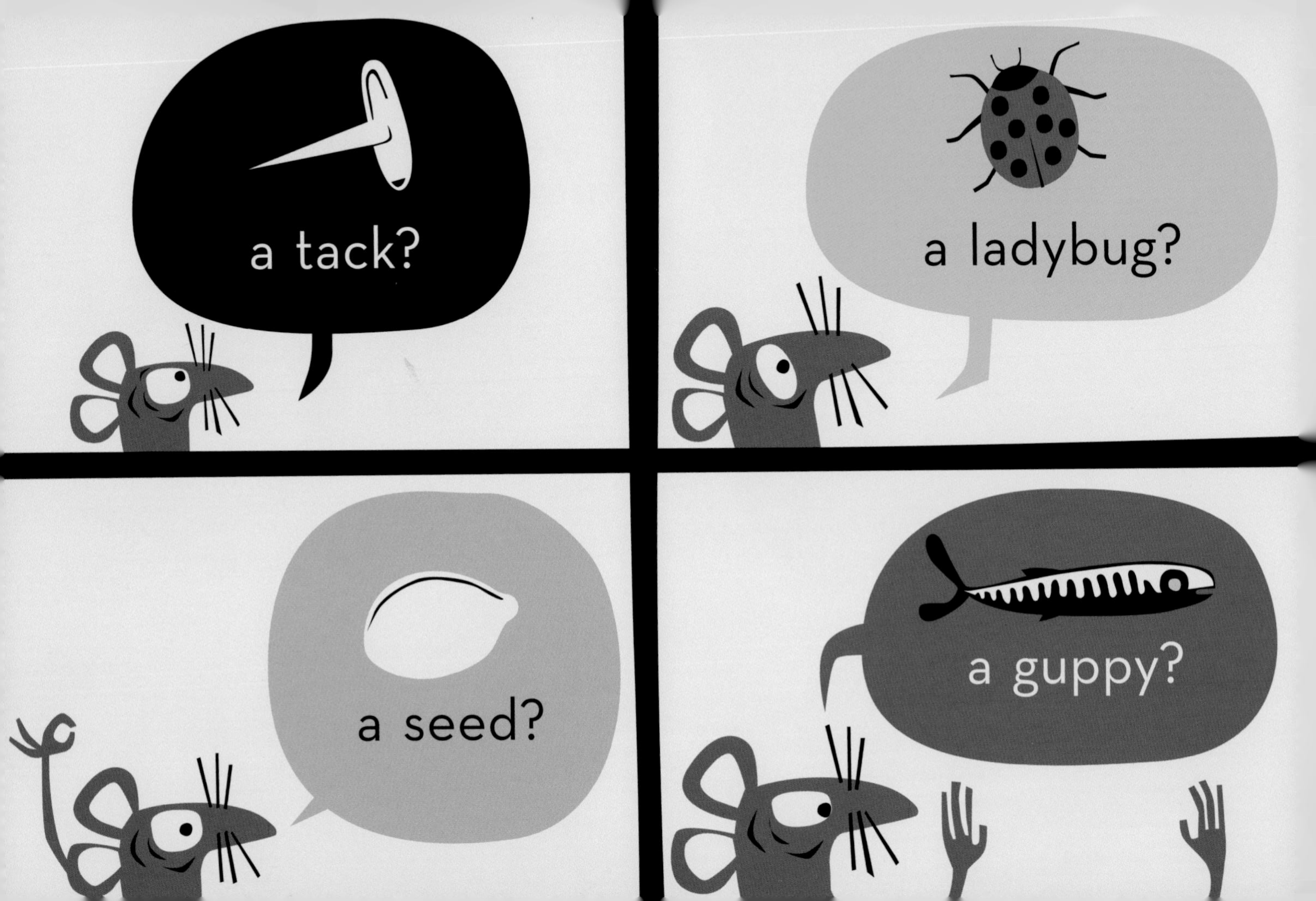
a tack?
a ladybug?
a seed?
a guppy?

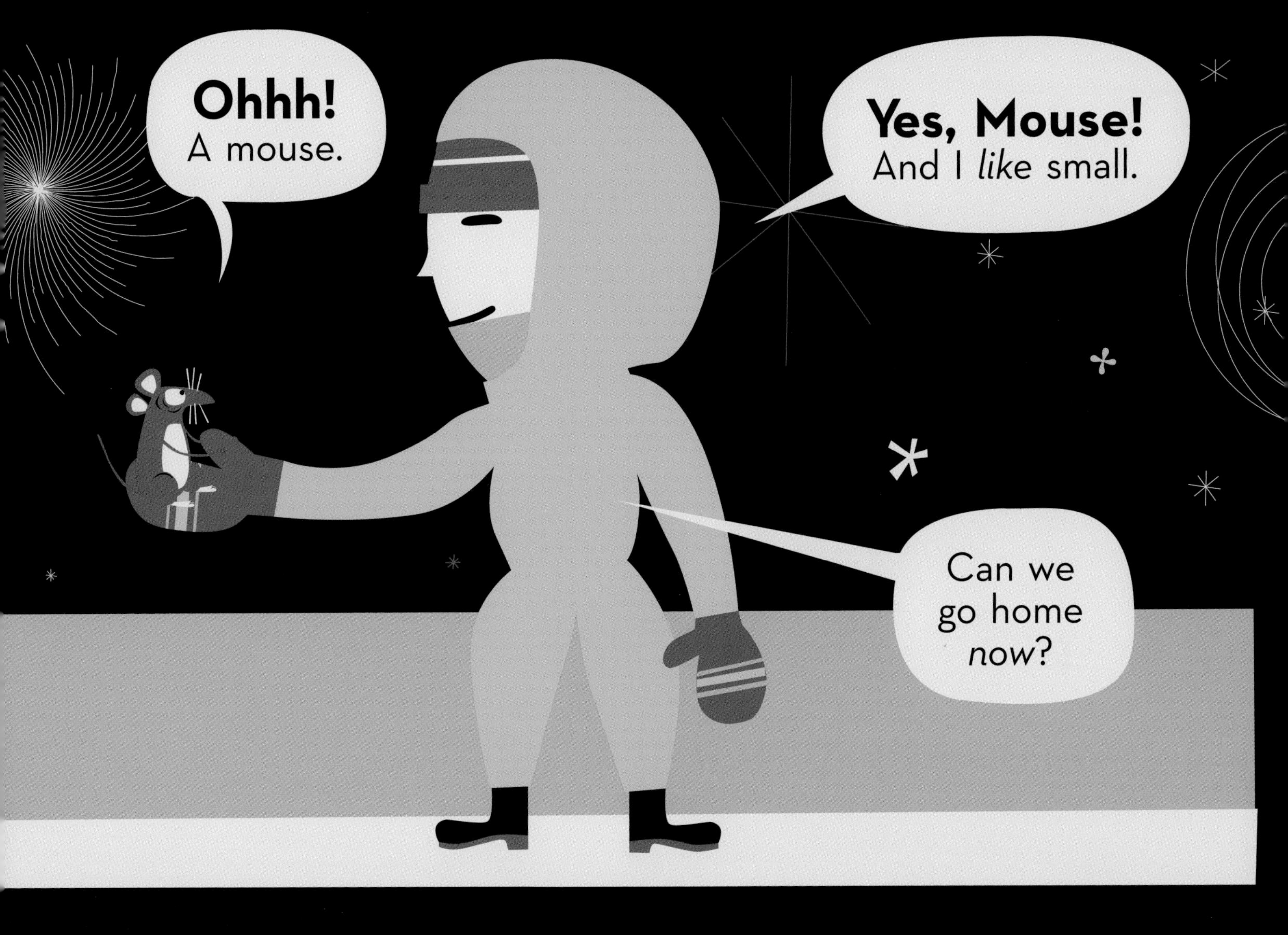
Ohhh! A mouse.
Yes, Mouse! And I *like* small.
Can we go home *now*?

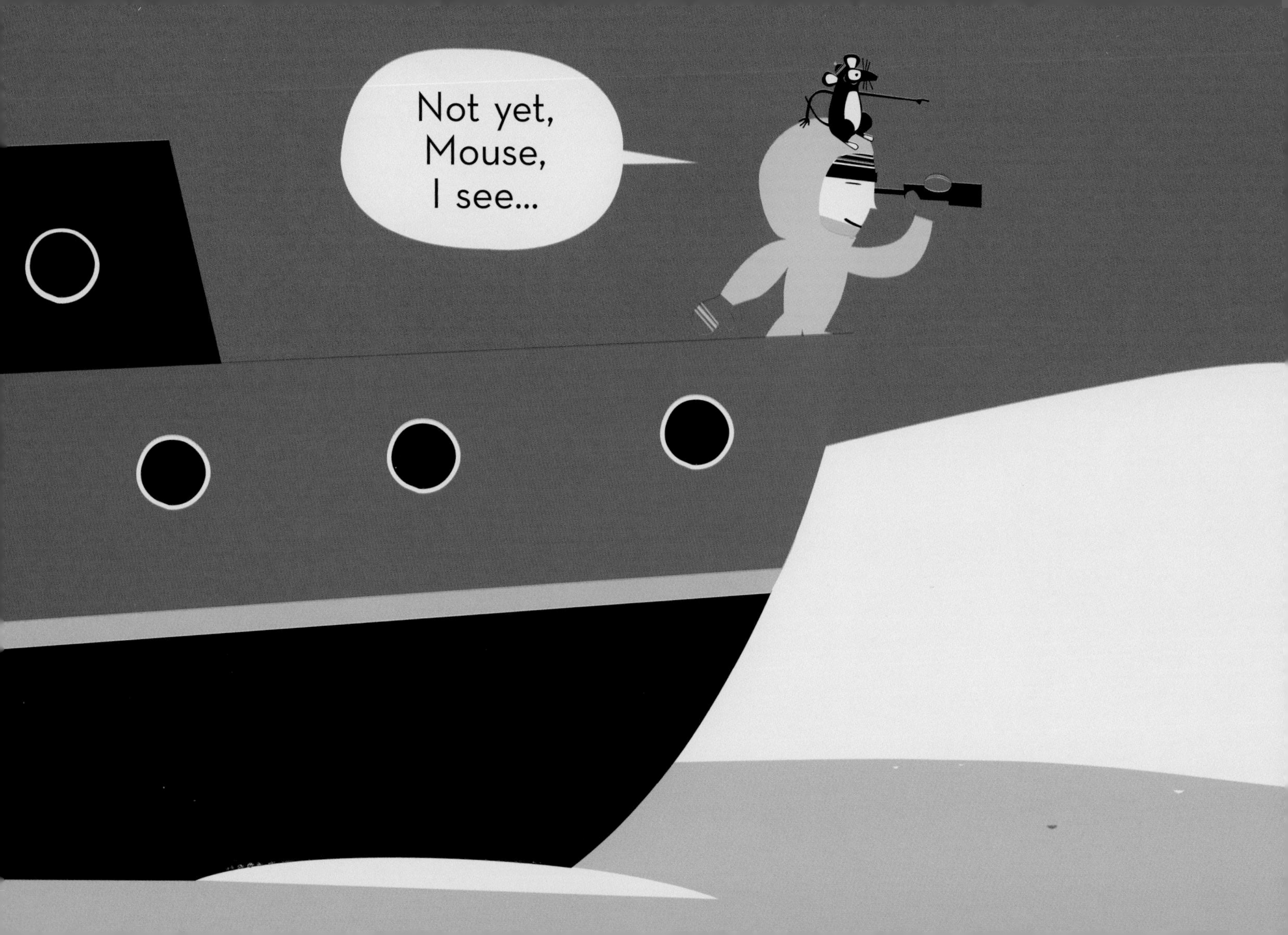
Not yet, Mouse, I see...

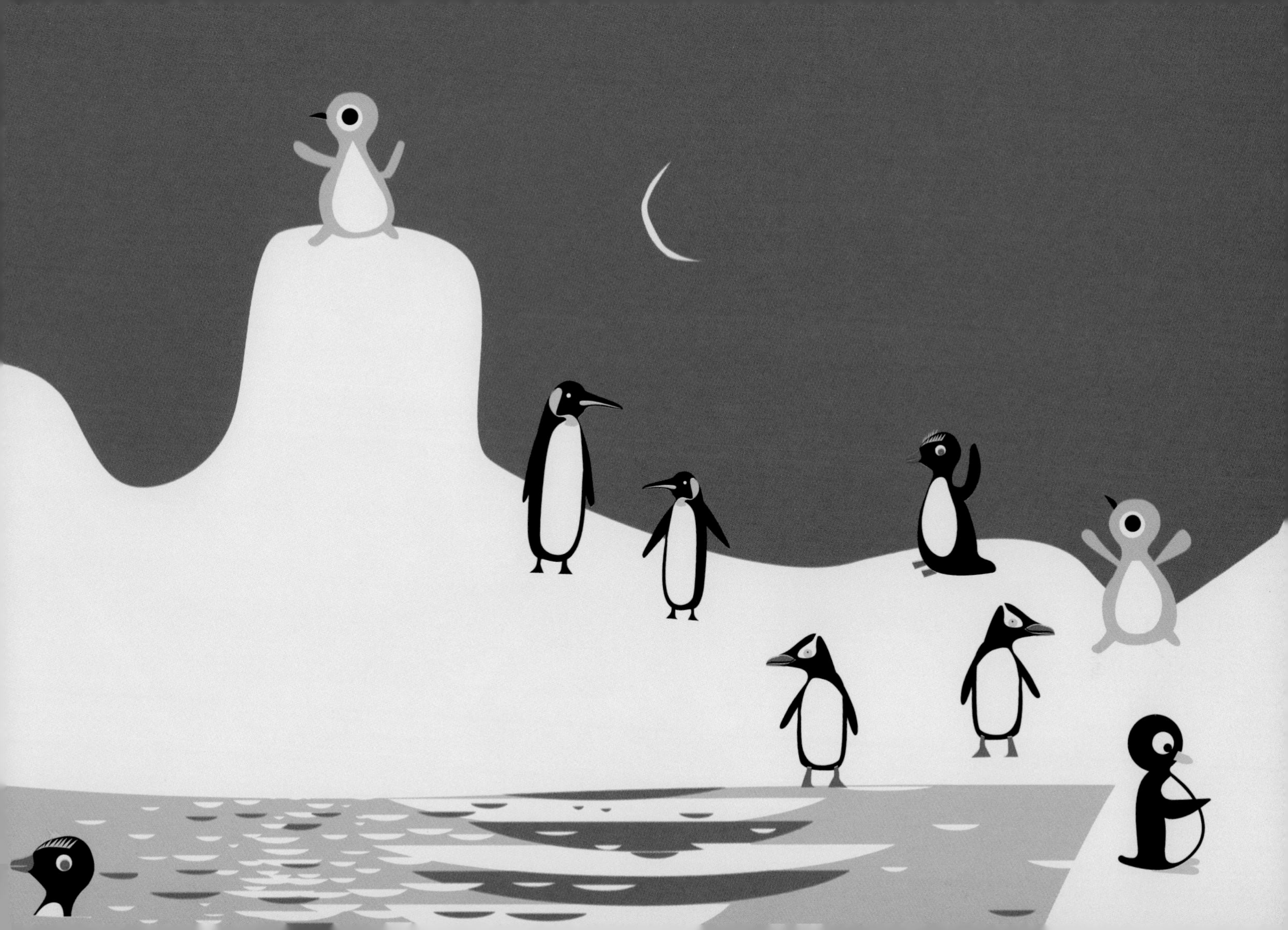

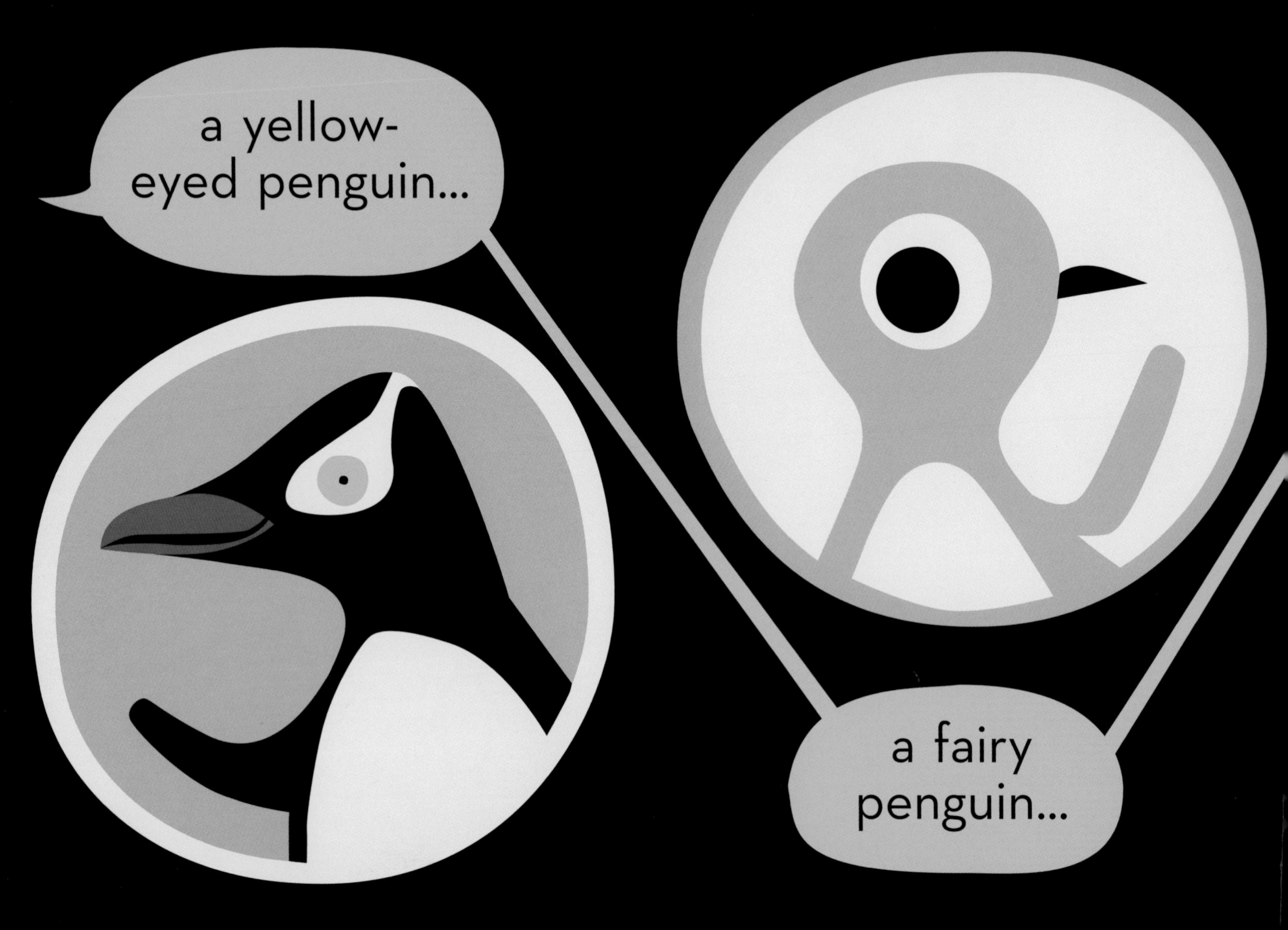
a yellow-eyed penguin...
a fairy penguin...

a macaroni penguin...

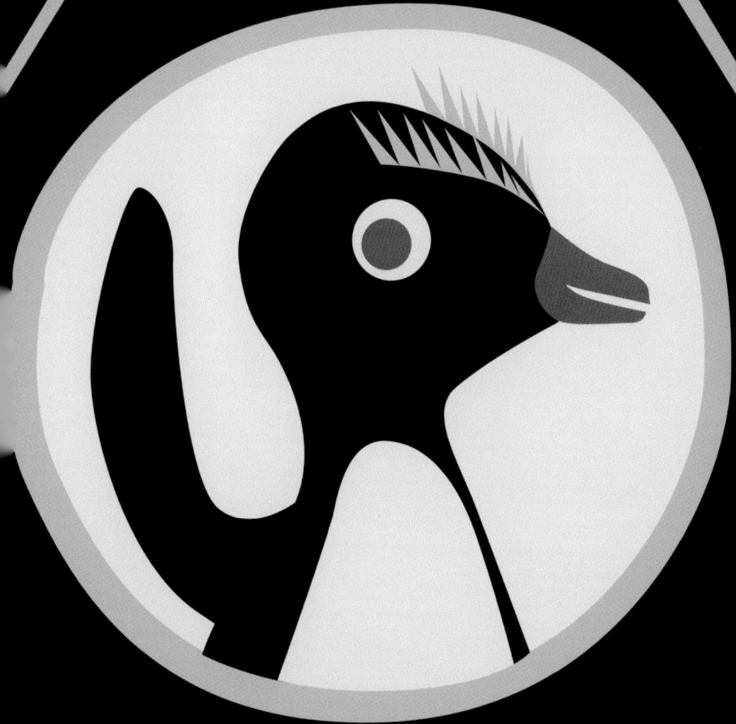

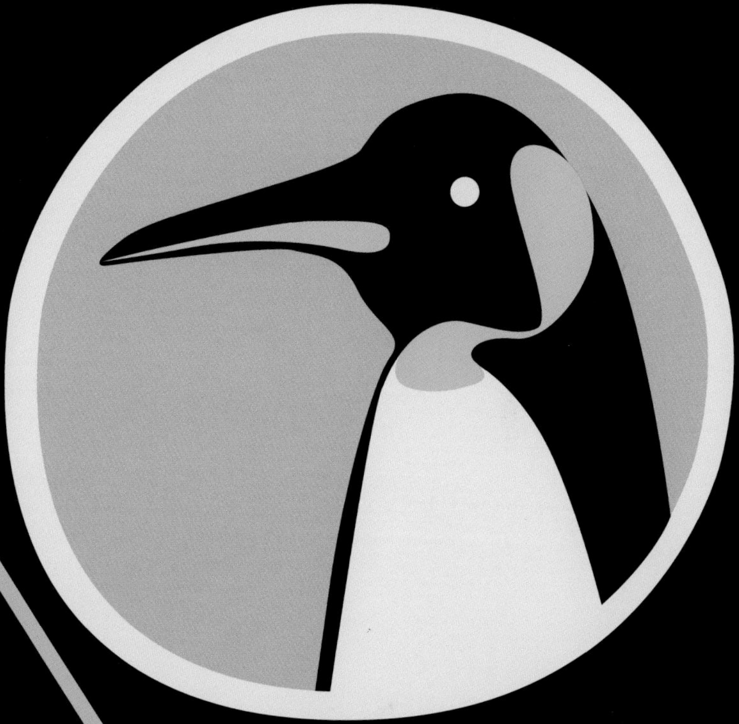

a king penguin...

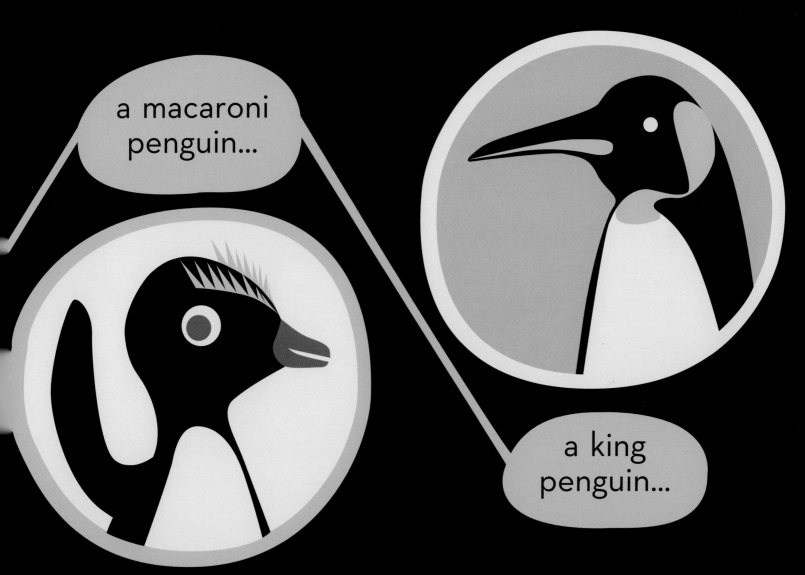

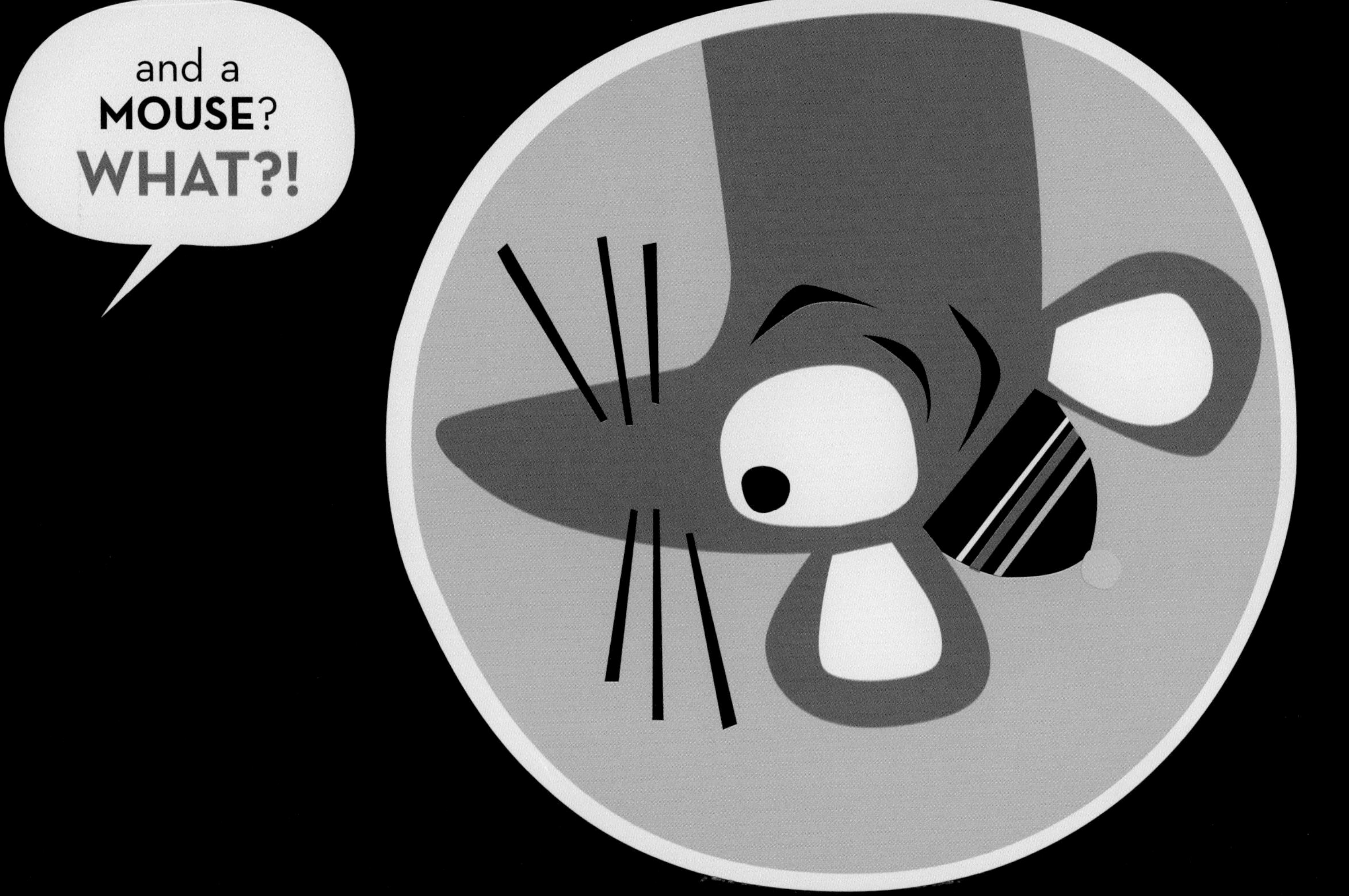
and a MOUSE? WHAT?!

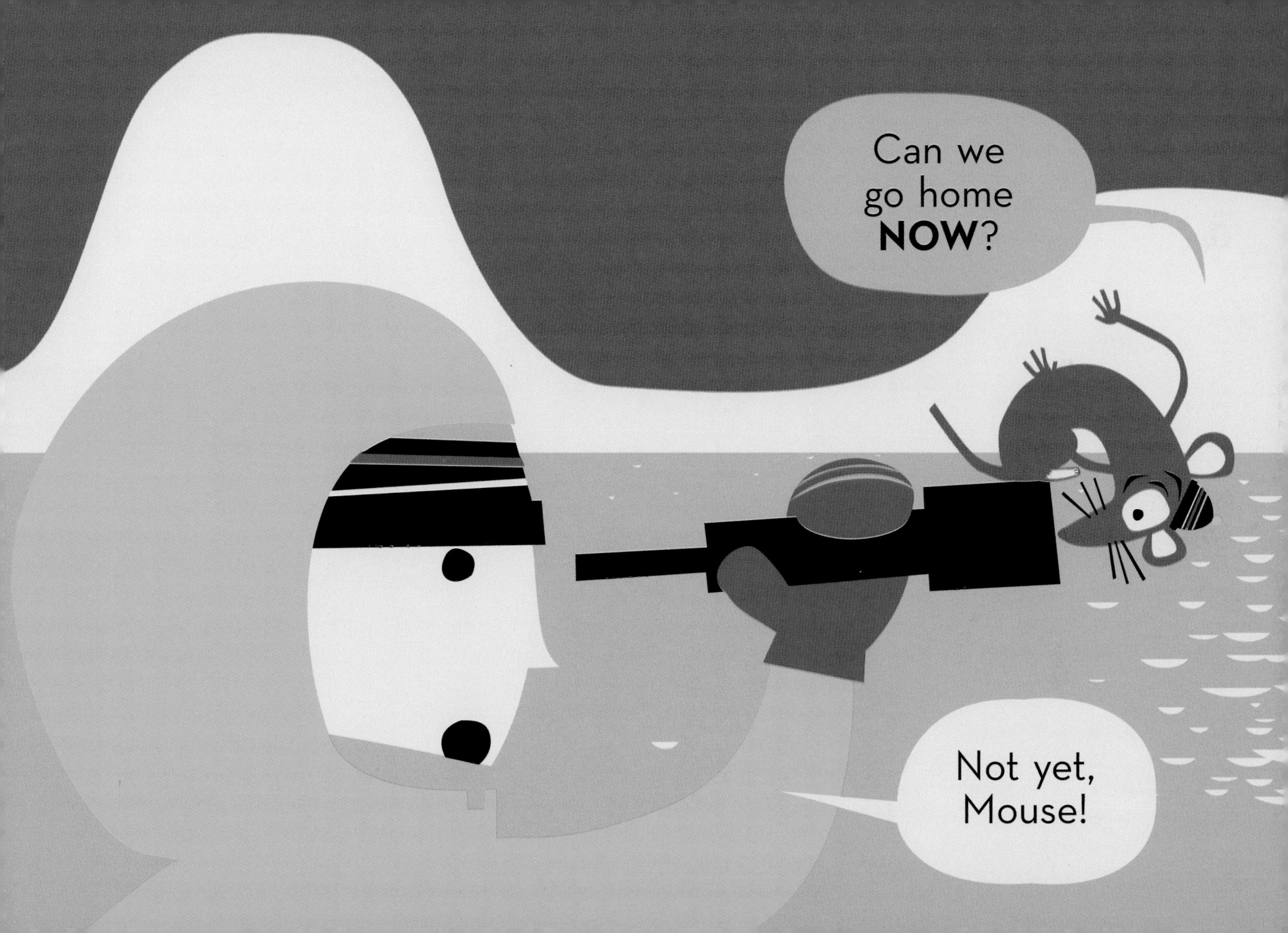
Can we go home **NOW**?
Not yet, Mouse!

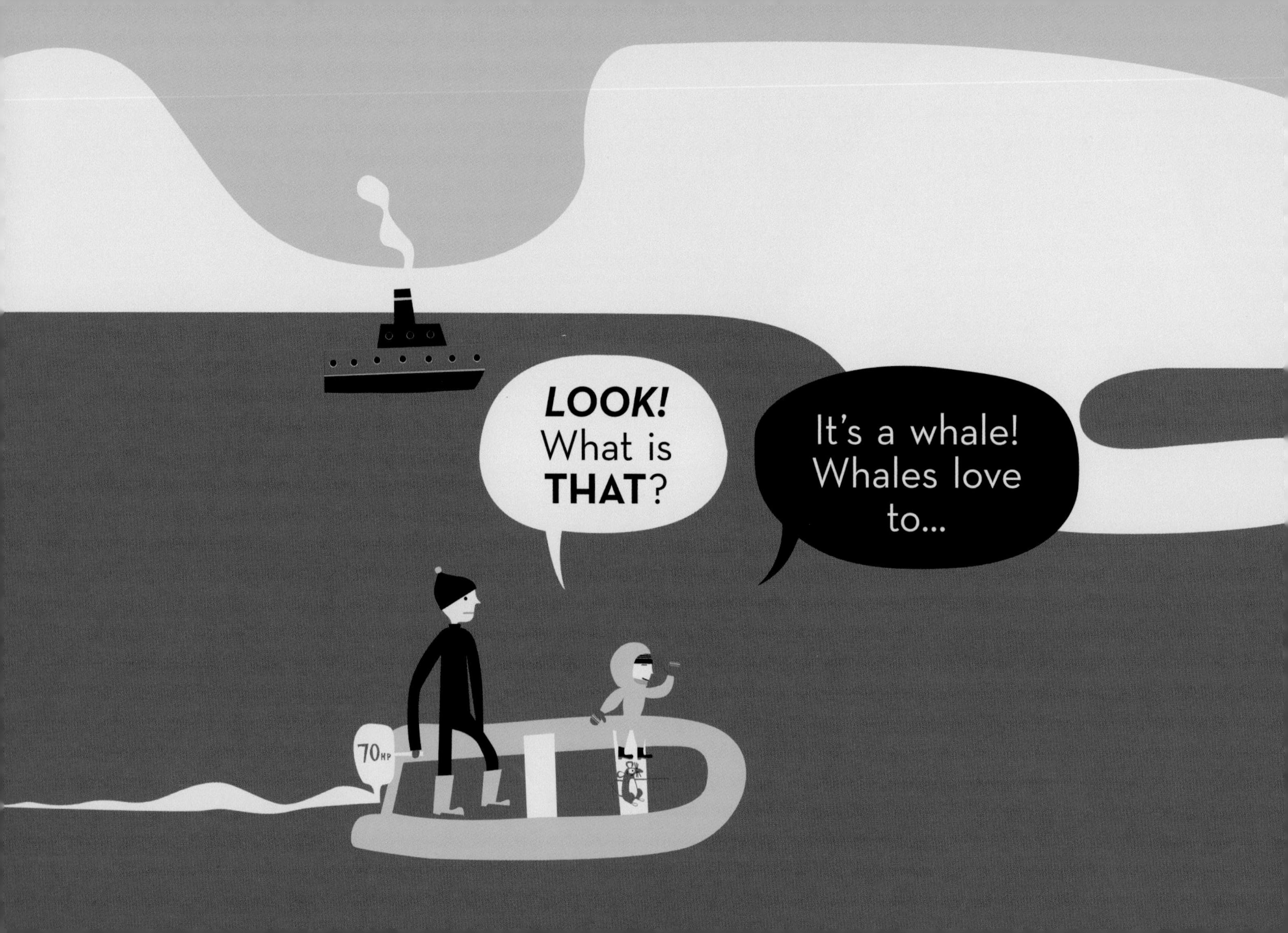
LOOK! What is **THAT**?
It's a whale! Whales love to...
70HP

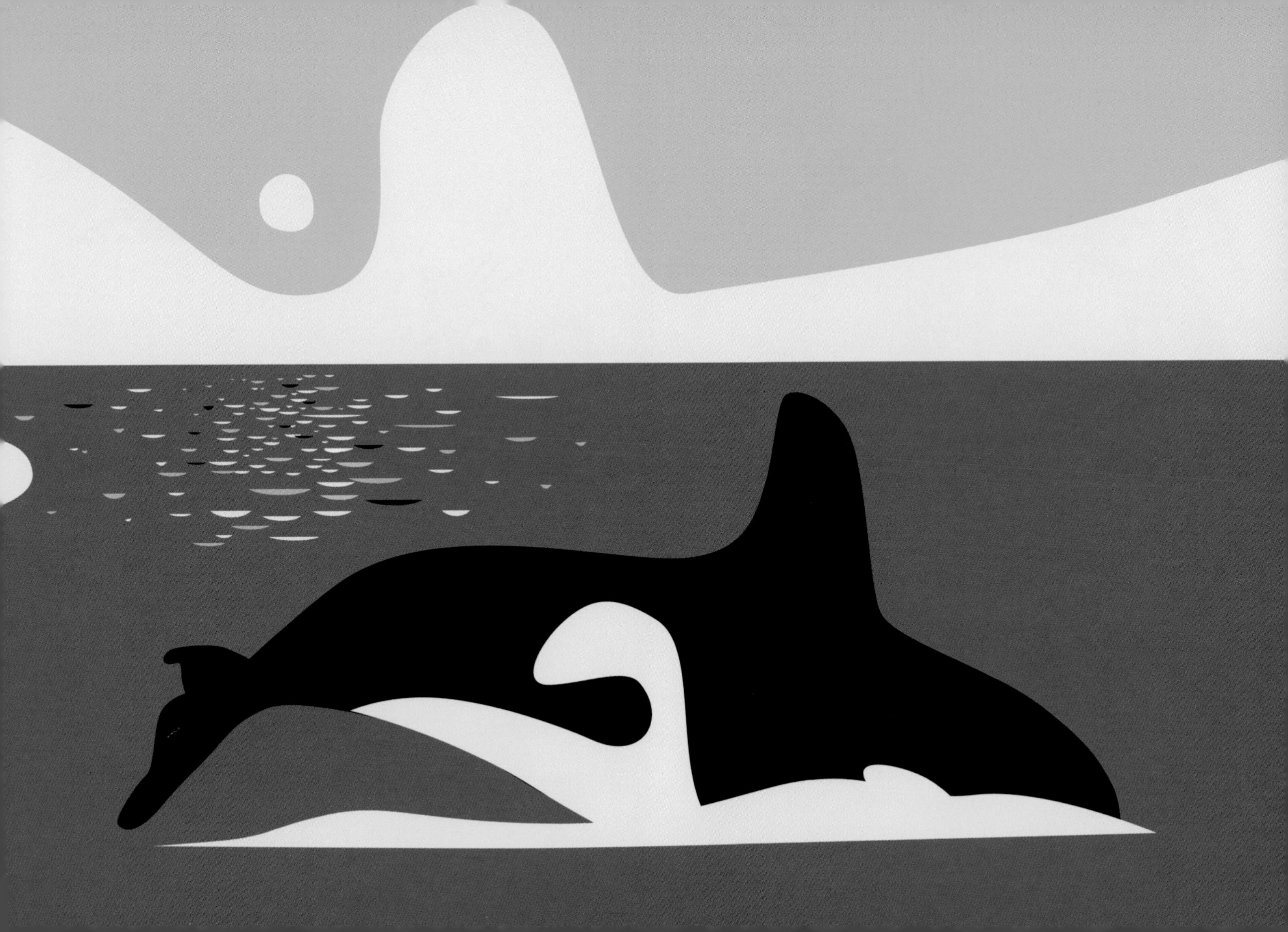

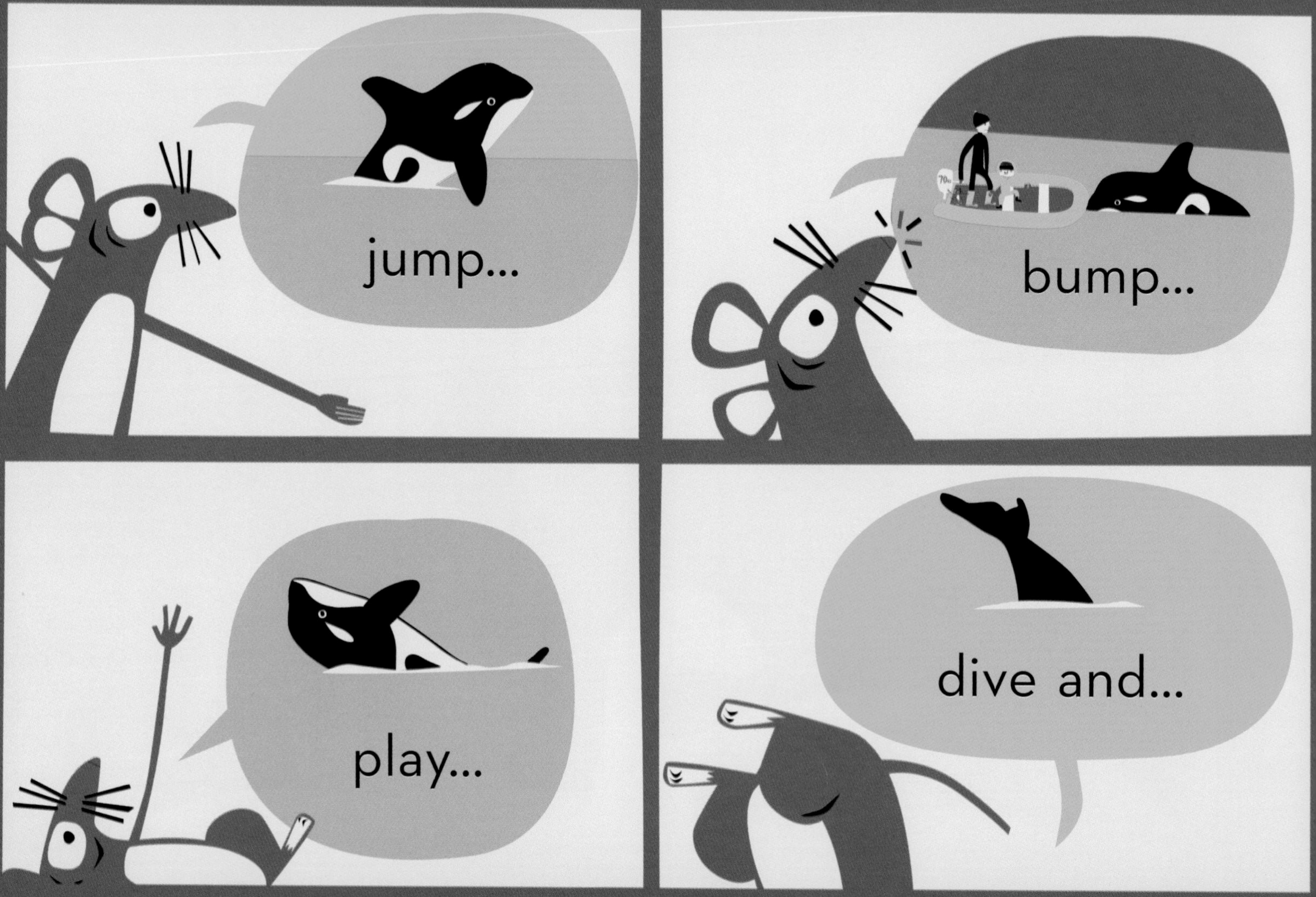
jump...
bump...
play...
dive and...

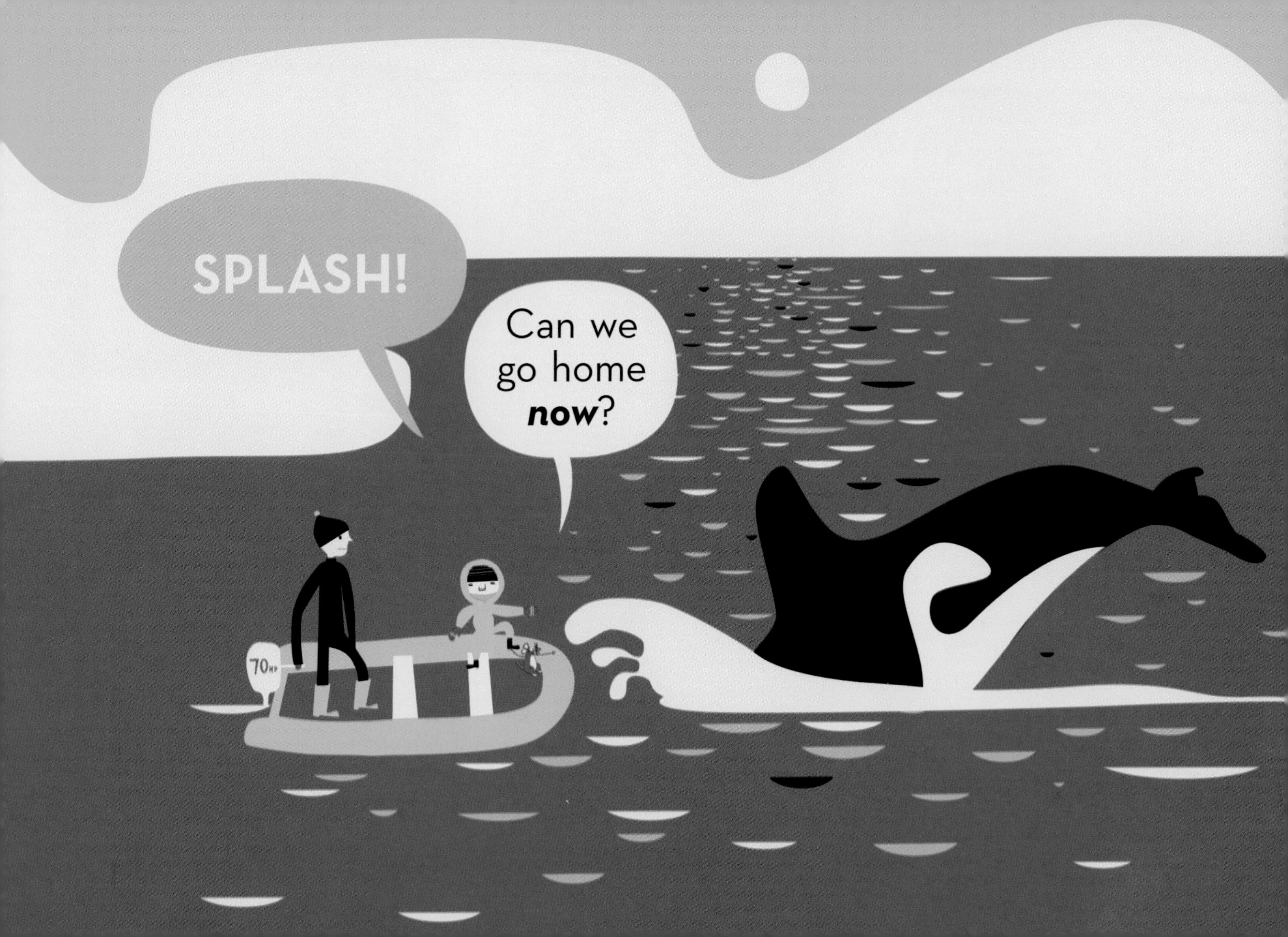
SPLASH!
Can we go home *now*?
70HP

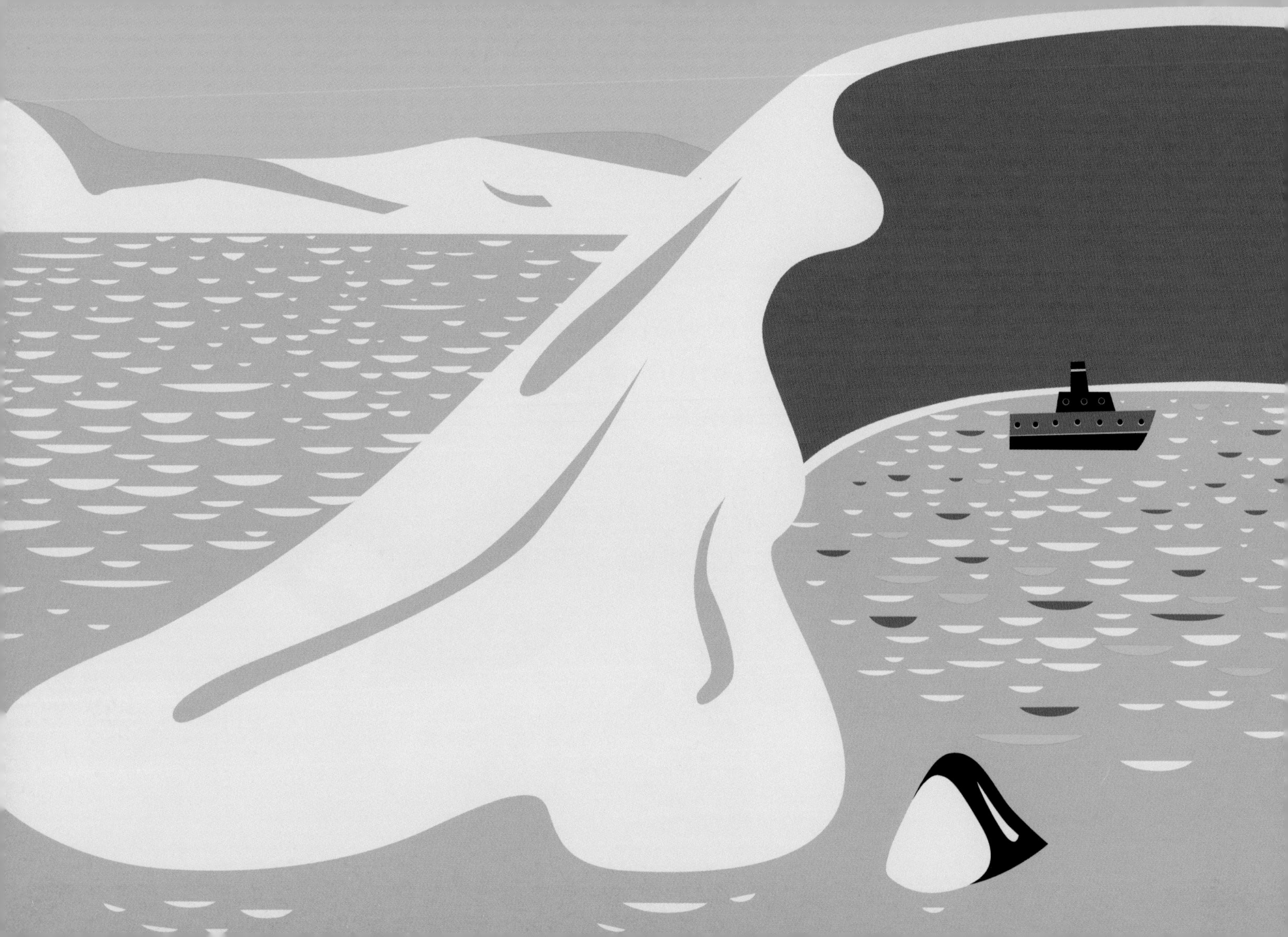

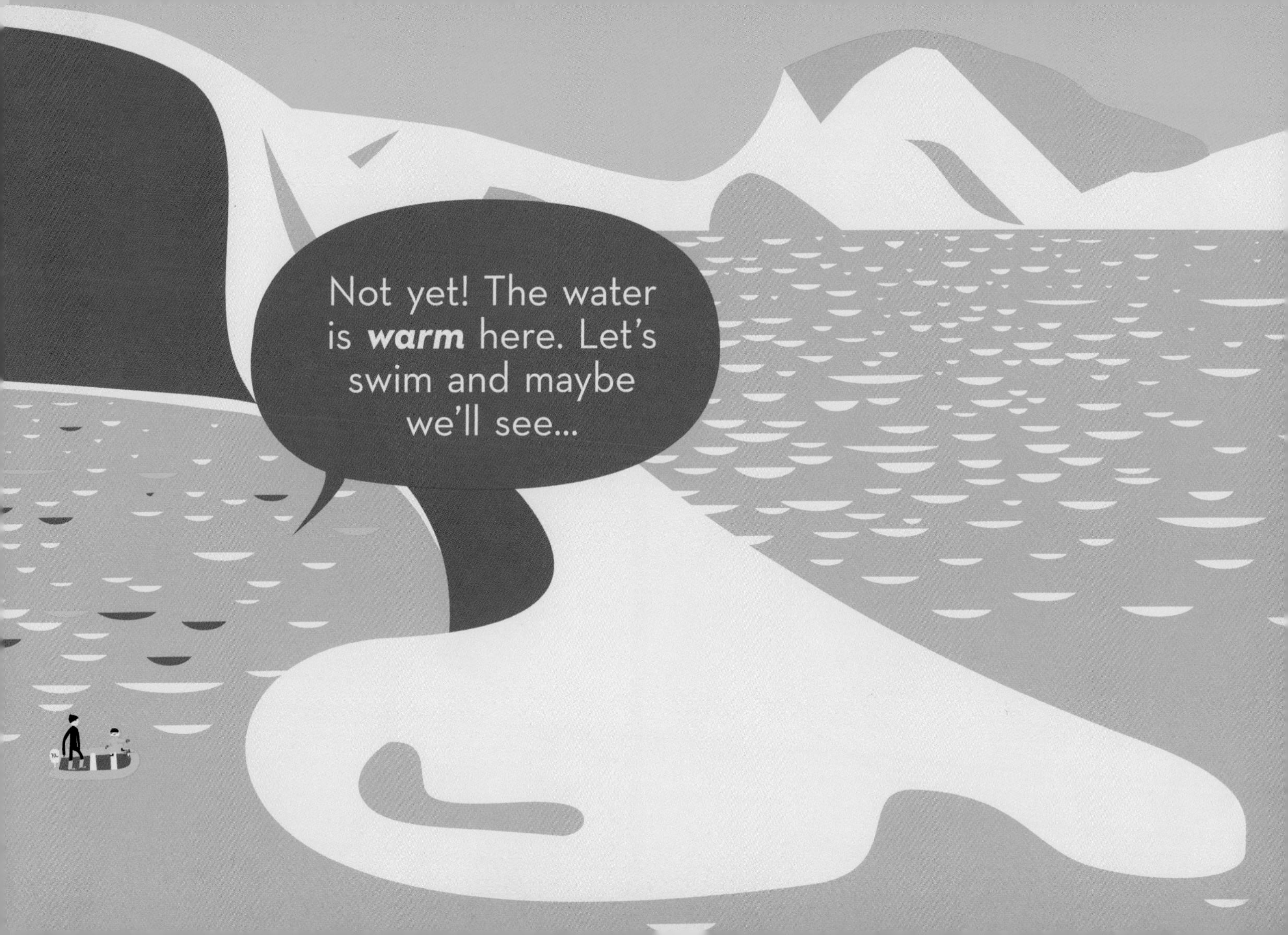
Not yet! The water is ***warm*** here. Let's swim and maybe we'll see...

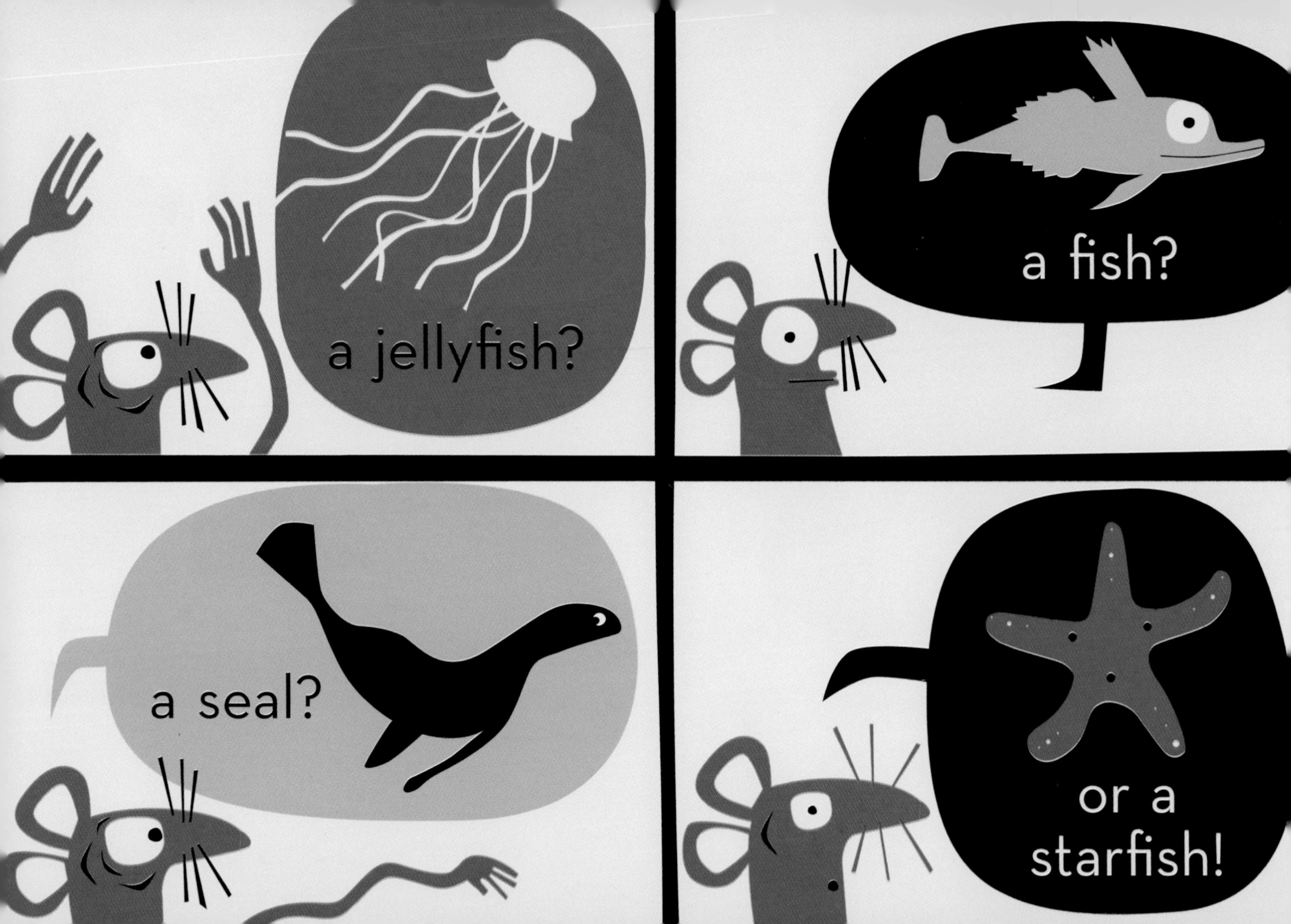
a jellyfish?
a fish?
a seal?
or a starfish!

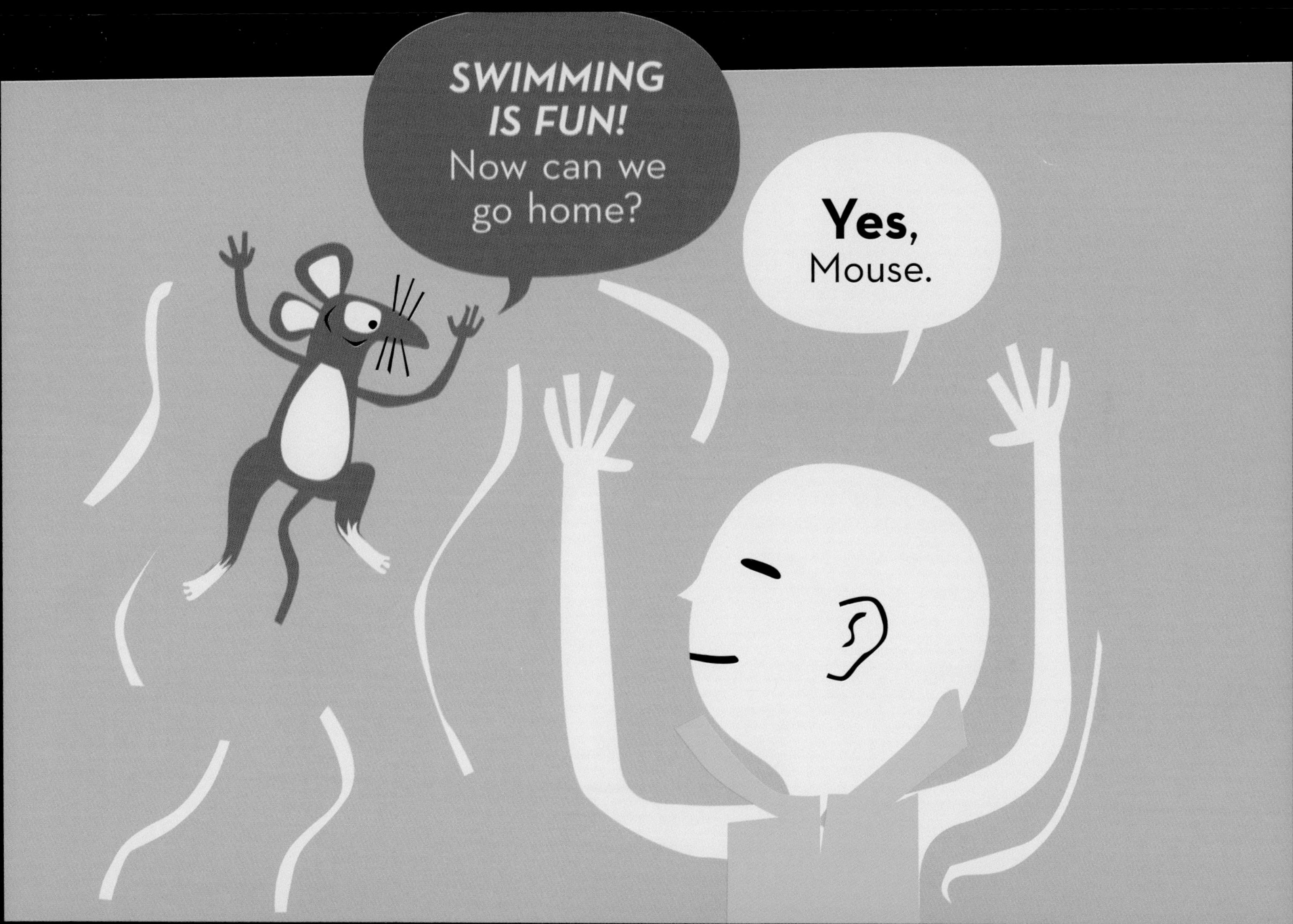
SWIMMING IS FUN! Now can we go home?
Yes, Mouse.

ABOUT THE AUTHOR

FRANK VIVA is an illustrator and designer who lives in Toronto, Canada. He is a cover artist for *The New Yorker* and sits on two college advisory boards. He is passionate about cooking, eating, and his daily bike ride to the office. His picture books, *Along a Long Road* and *A Long Way Away*, received widespread critical acclaim and *Along a Long Road* was chosen by *The New York Times* as one of its Ten Best Illustrated Books.

A Trip to the Bottom of the World is based on Frank's experiences aboard a Russian research vessel during a trip to the Antarctic Peninsula. On this once-in-a-lifetime adventure, while crossing the Drake Passage (the roughest waters in the world), he became sick—over and over and over again. But it was worth it. Once in Antarctica, he saw penguins and whales—and swam in the thermal waters of a submerged volcano. This chronicle of Frank's journey was just as fun to do—and much easier on his tummy.

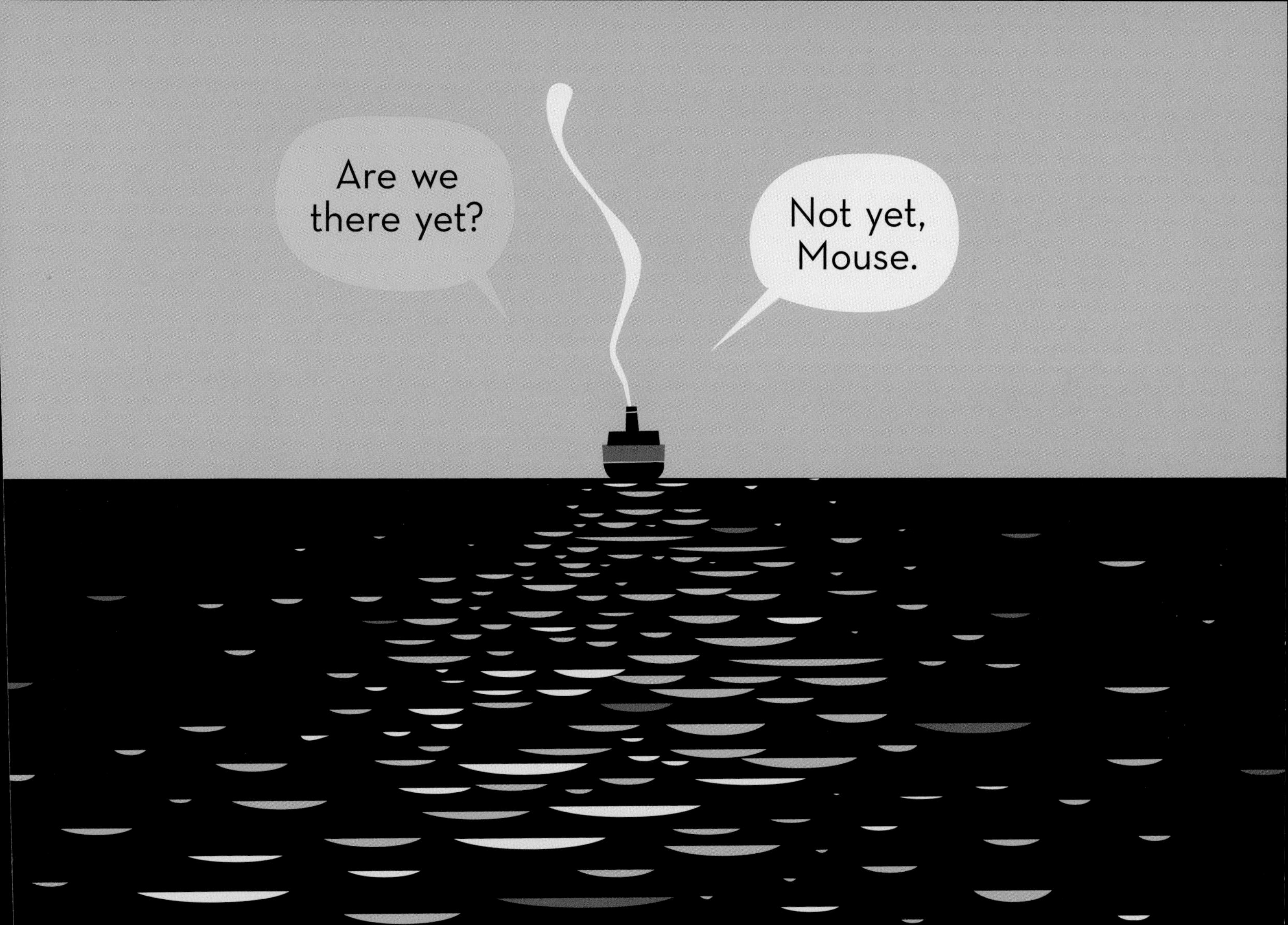
Are we there yet?
Not yet, Mouse.

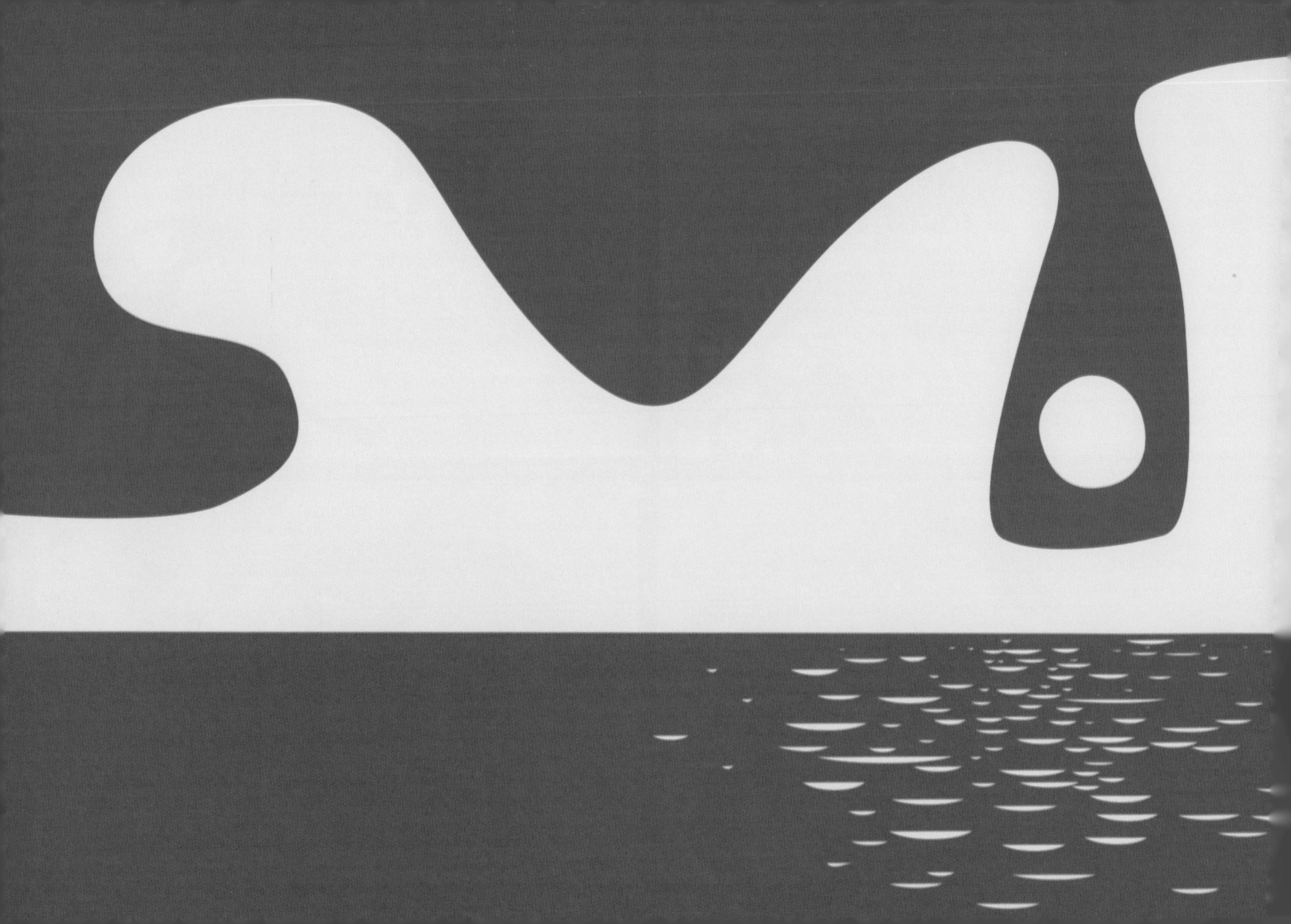

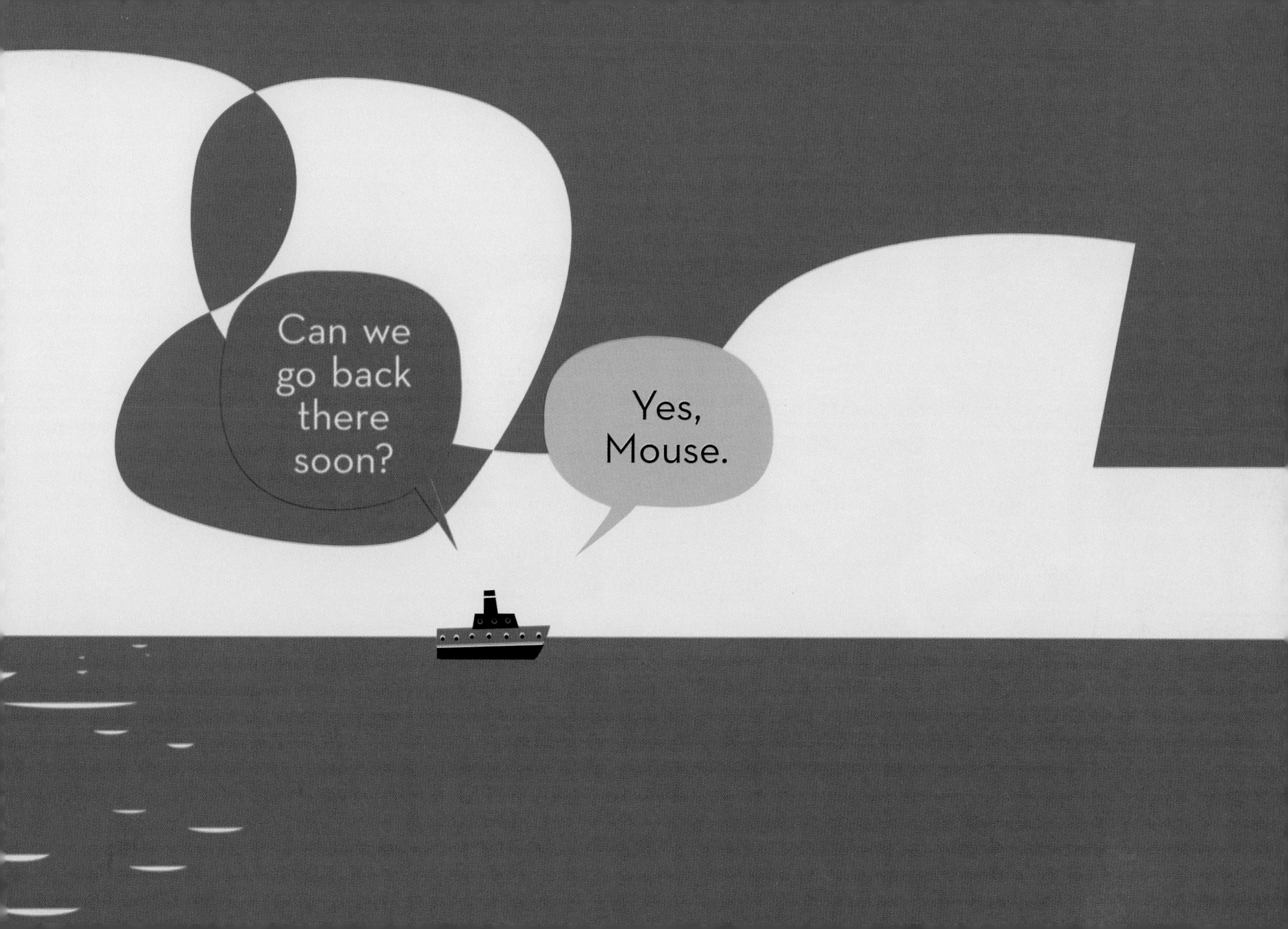
Can we go back there soon?
Yes, Mouse.

COLLECT THEM ALL!

LEVEL 1 FIRST COMICS FOR BRAND-NEW READERS

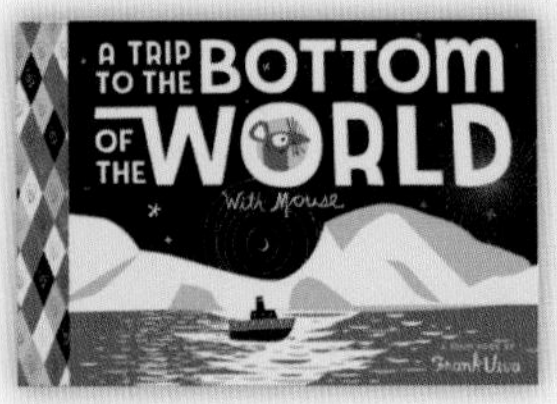
A TRIP TO THE BOTTOM OF THE WORLD
With Mouse
Frank Viva

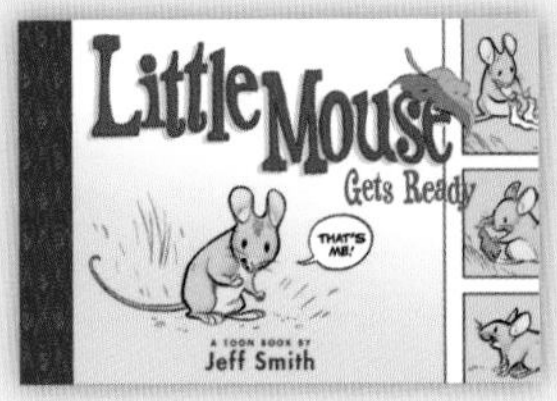
Little Mouse
Gets Ready
THAT'S ME!
A TOON BOOK BY
Jeff Smith

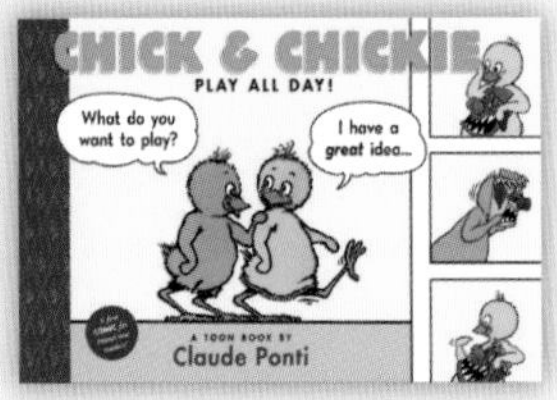
CHICK & CHICKIE
PLAY ALL DAY!
What do you want to play?
I have a great idea...
A TOON BOOK BY
Claude Ponti

LEVEL 2 EASY-TO-READ COMICS FOR EMERGING READERS

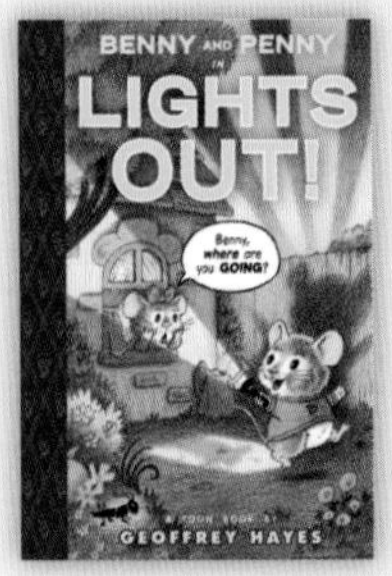
BENNY AND PENNY
LIGHTS OUT!
Benny, where are you GOING?
GEOFFREY HAYES

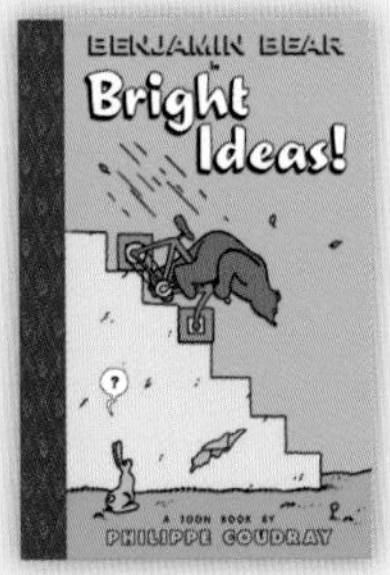
BENJAMIN BEAR
Bright Ideas!
A TOON BOOK BY
PHILIPPE COUDRAY

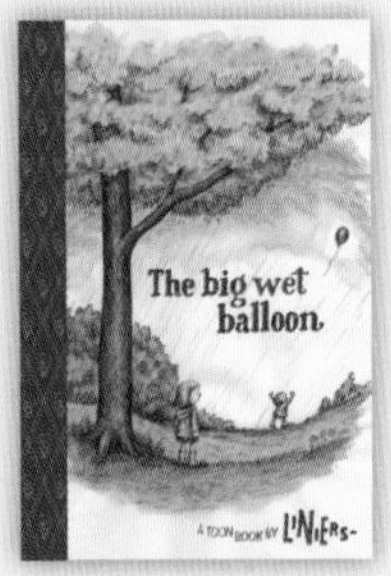
The big wet balloon
LINIERS

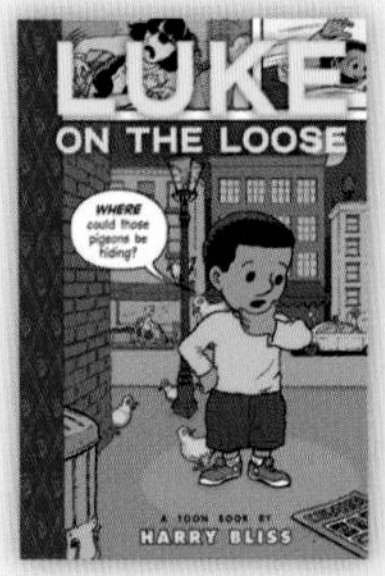
LUKE
ON THE LOOSE
A TOON BOOK BY
HARRY BLISS

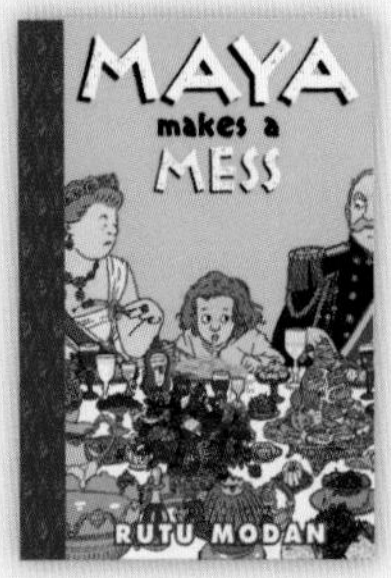
MAYA
makes a
MESS
RUTU MODAN

LEVEL 3 CHAPTER-BOOK COMICS FOR ADVANCED BEGINNERS

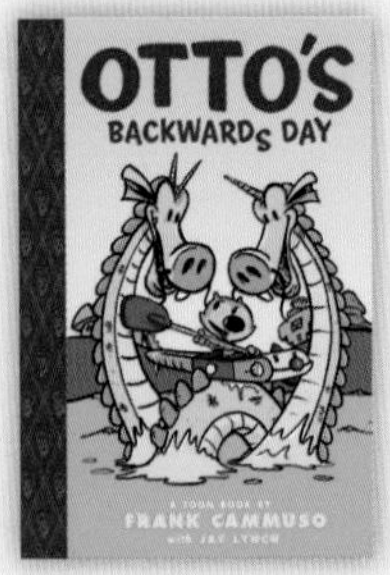
OTTO'S
BACKWARDS DAY
FRANK CAMMUSO

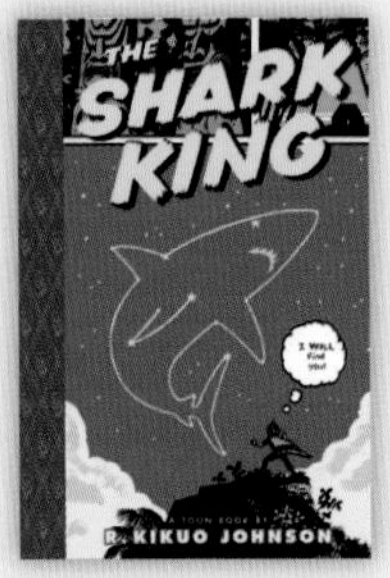
THE
SHARK
KING
KIKUO JOHNSON

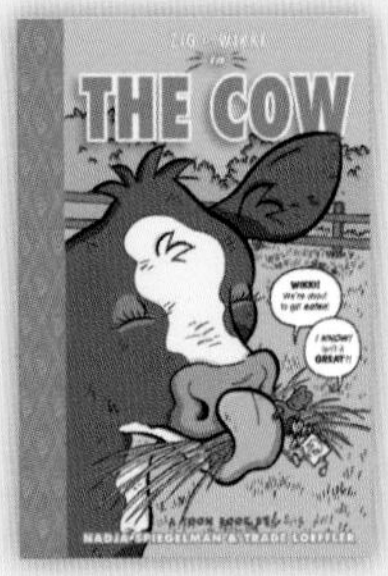
THE COW
NADJA SPIEGELMAN & TRADE LOEFFLER

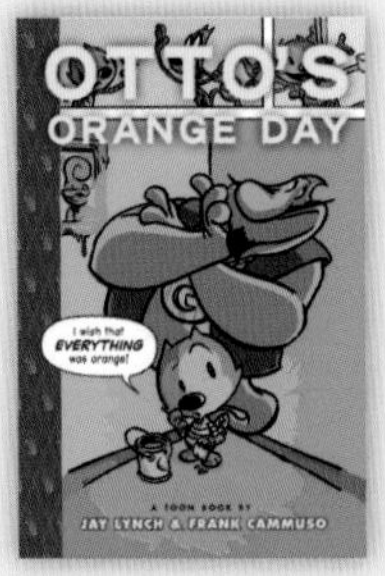
OTTO'S
ORANGE DAY
I wish that EVERYTHING was orange!
JAY LYNCH & FRANK CAMMUSO

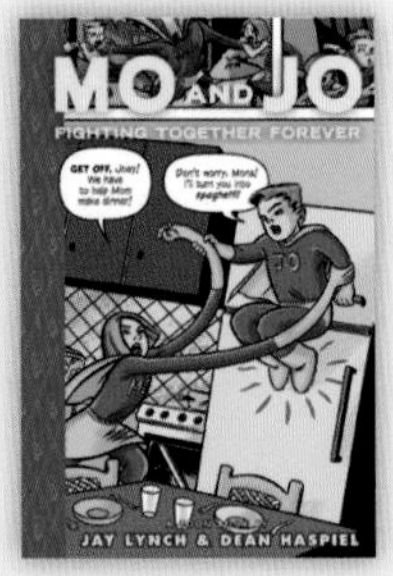
MO AND JO
FIGHTING TOGETHER FOREVER
JAY LYNCH & DEAN HASPIEL

TOON BOOKS

Set 1 • 10 hardcover books	**978-1-61479-147-8**
Benny and Penny in Just Pretend	978-1-61479-148-5
Benny and Penny in the Toy Breaker	978-1-61479-149-2
Chick & Chickie Play All Day!	978-1-61479-150-8
Jack and the Box	978-1-61479-151-5
Mo and Jo Fighting Together Forever	978-1-61479-152-2
Nina in That Makes Me Mad!	978-1-61479-153-9
Otto's Orange Day	978-1-61479-154-6
Silly Lilly and the Four Seasons	978-1-61479-155-3
Silly Lilly in What Will I Be Today?	978-1-61479-156-0
Zig and Wikki in Something Ate My Homework	978-1-61479-157-7
Set 2 • 8 hardcover books	**978-1-61479-298-7**
Benjamin Bear in Fuzzy Thinking	978-1-61479-299-4
Benny and Penny in the Big No-No!	978-1-61479-300-7
Little Mouse Gets Ready	978-1-61479-301-4
Luke on the Loose	978-1-61479-302-1
Maya Makes a Mess	978-1-61479-303-8
Patrick in a Teddy Bear's Picnic and Other Stories	978-1-61479-304-5
The Shark King	978-1-61479-305-2
Zig and Wikki in the Cow	978-1-61479-306-9
Set 3 • 6 hardcover books	**978-1-61479-422-6**
Benjamin Bear in Bright Ideas!	978-1-61479-423-3
Benny and Penny in Lights Out!	978-1-61479-424-0
The Big Wet Balloon	978-1-61479-425-7
Otto's Backwards Day	978-1-61479-426-4
Patrick Eats His Peas and Other Stories	978-1-61479-427-1
A Trip to the Bottom of the World with Mouse	978-1-61479-428-8